After the Frost

A CHRISTIAN ROMANCE
SEASONS OF FAITH BOOK 5

Milla Holt

REINBOK LIMITED
London, United Kingdom

Published by Reinbok Limited, 111 Wolsey Drive, Kingston Upon Thames, Greater London, KT2 5DR

Cover by 100 Covers

Book Layout ©2017 BookDesignTemplates.com

After the Frost / Milla Holt. -- 1st ed.

ISBN 978-1-913416-24-9

Print ISBN 978-1-913416-25-6

WELCOME TO THE MOSAIC COLLECTION

W E A R E S I S T E R S, A beautiful mosaic united by the love of God through the blood of Christ.

Each month The Mosaic Collection releases one or more faith-based novels or anthologies exploring our theme, Family by His Design, and sharing stories that feature diverse, God-designed families. Stories range from mystery and women's fiction to comedic and literary fiction. We hope you'll join our Mosaic family as we explore together what truly defines a family.

If you're like us, loneliness and suffering have touched your life in ways you never imagined; but Dear One, while you may feel alone in your suffering—whatever it is—you are never alone!

Learn more about The Mosaic Collection at
www.mosaiccollectionbooks.com
Join our Reader Community, too!
www.facebook.com/groups/TheMosaicCollection

BOOKS IN THE MOSAIC COLLECTION

When Mountains Sing by Stacy Monson

Unbound by Eleanor Bertin

The Red Journal by Deb Elkink

A Beautiful Mess by Brenda S. Anderson

Hope is Born: A Mosaic Christmas Anthology

More Than Enough by Lorna Seilstad

The Road to Happenstance by Janice L. Dick

This Side of Yesterday by Angela D. Meyer

Lost Down Deep by Sara Davison

The Mischief Thief by Johnnie Alexander

Before Summer's End: Stories to Touch the Soul

Tethered by Eleanor Bertin

Calm Before the Storm by Janice L. Dick

Heart Restoration by Regina Rudd Merrick

Pieces of Granite by Brenda S. Anderson

Watercolors by Lorna Seilstad

A Star Will Rise: A Mosaic Christmas Anthology II

Eye of the Storm by Janice L. Dick

Totally Booked: A Book Lover's Companion

Lifelines by Eleanor Bertin

To my husband, who is my biggest cheerleader

Chapter One

REIDUN NORBERG STAYED WELL below the speed limit as her truck approached the sharp bend in the road around Berghaven Harbor.

There was no need to hurry home from work when all that awaited her was an empty house and a TV dinner.

It was still technically summer, but, clearly, the weather couldn't read the calendar. A cold, driving rain fell from the brooding low-hanging clouds as though an October day had strayed into August.

Reidun adjusted the heating on the dashboard. She'd make sure that TV dinner was a hot curry.

She rounded the bend, gently depressing the brakes on her truck. What was this? A white car, its hazard lights flashing, was nestled in the roadside ditch.

Reidun's heart lurched. Were they all right? She pulled up a safe distance ahead and set her own hazard lights on.

She jumped out of her truck, pulling her hood over her head as she approached the car. It was a white Ford Focus.

Her stomach knotted up as she got closer, and she reached for her phone in case she needed to call for help.

The driver's side window rolled down, and a man looked up at her. A very handsome man. His salt and pepper hair framed a face that was probably too perfect when he was younger, but had now weathered to a well-worn ruggedness.

She leaned forward. "Are you all right?"

"Yes, we're all fine," he said, revealing teeth that were as flawless as his face. "I can't get out of this ditch, but I've called a tow truck. We're waiting for them to show up, but I appreciate your stopping to check on us."

We? She looked beyond him into the car. An older woman sat in the passenger seat, fiddling with a cellphone. Two strikingly beautiful chil-

dren, a boy and a girl, both blond-haired and blue-eyed, stared back at her from the back seat.

The little girl leaned forward. "Dad slid into the ditch and now we can't get out." She spoke in English, rather than Norwegian. Were they tourists? But their dad's dialect sounded like he was from up here in the far north of Norway.

Reidun marshaled up her English. "That happens to many people on this road, especially when it's been raining all day. I'm glad you're okay." She turned back to the man. "You know, I've got towing equipment in my truck. I'm happy to help."

His eyes rounded. "Um, thanks, but I think I'd better wait for the pro—I mean, for the towing company."

He'd been about to say "the professionals." Fair enough. She couldn't blame him for refusing help from a random person. "All right," she said. "But while you wait, it might be a good idea to put out your hazard warning triangle. This is a notorious blind corner, and I'd hate for someone else to join you in that ditch."

He stiffened, a deep red staining his cheeks. "I'm not sure I have one."

"Of course you have one, unless you removed it. Every car does." She hesitated, remembering his English-speaking children. "It's been required by law in Norway for almost twenty years."

His gaze slid away from her face. "I wouldn't know where to look, to be honest."

"Let's check in your trunk."

He stepped out, revealing a tall, well-built frame, two or three inches taller than her five foot ten.

She followed him to the back of the car, and he popped the trunk open. It was full of luggage, with fresh baggage tags attached. Had they just arrived in Norway?

She pointed to the back corner of his trunk. "I used to have a Ford like this. Your hazard triangle is probably under the mat over there, but you'll have to take out some of your bags."

He removed the suitcases. Sure enough, there was a tab on the mat.

He opened the compartment and pulled out a small red oblong case. His eyebrows drew together as he stared at it, turning it round in his smooth hands for a long moment.

Reidun crossed her arms. Didn't he know how to set it up?

"It might be a good idea to place a second one because of the blind corner," she said. "I'll lend you mine."

She jogged to her truck and grabbed her hazard triangle. She walked up to him and unzipped the red pouch, then unfolded the triangle, suppressing a smile as he surreptitiously watched and copied her motions to set up his own.

"I'll put mine down the road and you can place yours in front of your car," she said.

With her hazard triangle about thirty-five meters from his car, anyone approaching would get a heads-up and be on the lookout.

When she got back to him, he was leaning on his car and frowning at his phone.

He looked at her. "The tow company's estimated arrival time is seventy minutes. Up from fifty-five."

Reidun winced. "That's probably because they're based over in Havdal. And they're probably finishing up with other call-outs before they get to yours."

The passenger window slid down, and the little girl poked her head through. "Dad, I'm hungry. And Chase needs to poop."

The man pushed a hand into his hair, his gaze going from his daughter to his phone.

Reidun knew little about children, but she did know that when they needed to go, they needed to go. She held up both hands, palms facing outward. "Listen, no pressure, but I've towed a few cars before. I've got a recovery strap in my truck, and we could get you out of that ditch in under fifteen minutes."

He stared at her, shaking his head. "You just happen to have towing equipment sitting in your car? Are you a mechanic or something?"

"No, I'm actually a plumber. But when you live in the far north, it makes sense to be prepared for trouble. Especially when the nearest towing company might be hours away." Her face heated. Did he think she was criticizing him? "No offense," she added. "My friends used to tease me for having a recovery strap until one of them got stuck in a snowdrift."

"No offense taken."

She watched the internal debate that played across his features.

Finally, he said, "Thanks. I accept your offer. Things are getting pretty desperate for my son. What should we do?"

She clapped her hands together. "First, move both hazard triangles to the middle of the road to stop oncoming traffic. I'm going to need all this space to maneuver. When you've done that, I'll get everything hooked up."

While he went to move the triangles, she crouched behind his car to see what she had to work with. Thank goodness. It had the recovery points she needed. This should be straightforward.

Placing the second triangle, he called out to her. "What are you going to do?"

"I'll tow your car backward onto the road. You need to get inside it and keep it in neutral, with the brakes on."

The lady's voice floated out from his car. She spoke in English, too. "Steinar, what's going on? What's that woman doing?"

Ah, so his name was Steinar. A nice, solid, Norwegian name.

He walked back to his car. "She's going to tow us out."

"Are you sure it's okay? I thought you'd called a tow truck."

"I think she knows what she's doing," Steinar said. "It can't hurt to try."

The conversation faded as Reidun went back into her truck and maneuvered it into place.

Steinar was back in his car, so she spoke to him through the window. "I've attached my recovery strap to your car and hooked it up to my truck.

We should have you out in no time. Thankfully, this isn't a very busy road, so we're not holding up any traffic."

But as she jumped into her truck, a vehicle slowed and stopped on the other side of her warning triangle. She flashed her lights and waved at the waiting driver. She'd better get this done fast before any other cars came along.

She figured the fastest way to get Steinar's car out was if she drove directly across the road. She edged her truck forward.

Looking over her shoulder and through her rear view windshield, she glimpsed two vehicles lining up and waiting.

Reidun pushed on the gas pedal. Just a little more should do it.

She sensed the tension in her tow strap slacking, and eased off the gas. Looking over her shoulder, Reidun puffed out a relieved breath. Steinar's vehicle was completely out of the ditch. Thank God!

She ran up to him, giving him a thumbs-up, which he returned with a grin.

"Don't drive off just yet—I need to unhook you," she said, recalling the teenage driver she'd towed once who had attempted to pull away while still attached to her truck.

In a minute, she unhooked her strap and moved her truck to the side of the road.

The waiting vehicles drove past, with one driver giving her a cheery wave.

Steinar walked up to her with her hazard triangle. "I can't thank you enough. For everything."

She shrugged, taking the triangle out of his hand. "It's what people in Berghaven do. Anyone else would have gladly helped."

"Good thing this is our new home, then. Thanks once again." He glanced back at his car. "I'd better go before my son has a major accident. Bye."

He went off and Reidun started her engine. A few meters down the road, she remembered that she hadn't asked his full name. And he hadn't asked for hers. Ah, well. Perhaps she'd see him around town.

Chapter Two

STEINAR JAKOBSEN BREATHED A prayer of thanks as he clicked his seatbelt into place.

"Everything all right?" his mother-in-law, Doris Montague, asked. "You shortened my life by five years when you skidded off the road. I told you that you took that corner too fast."

Steinar gritted his teeth.

He knew he'd been an idiot. After working all night to set up a digital marketing campaign for a client, he was in no shape to make the hour-long round trip to the airport to pick up Doris and his children. Falling asleep at the wheel, he might have drifted into oncoming traffic. Thank God he'd only ended up in a ditch.

He glanced in his rearview mirror to steal a glimpse of his children. He'd never forgive himself if he'd hurt them through a careless mistake.

Steinar started the car and eased back onto the road.

"Yay, we're not stuck anymore," Chase yelled.

His twin sister Mya said, "That tow truck lady was really cool."

She was indeed. And Steinar hadn't even asked her name. He definitely wasn't firing on all cylinders today. But their Good Samaritan rescuer said she lived in Berghaven, and it was such a small town that they would probably run into her at some point.

Built like an Amazon, with smooth dark skin and short curly hair, she wasn't the kind to blend into a crowd. And how many Black female plumbers could there be in the far north of Norway?

Not that he'd gotten to know many people in town. Since moving here a couple of months ago, he'd been holed up in his house working on a client's demanding, deadline-driven project. He hadn't even had time to find a church.

Now that his children were here, though, this place would feel more like home.

"Are you excited to see the house?" he asked them.

"Yeah," Mya said. "Are we nearly there?"

"I need the bathroom," Chase added.

"We'll be there in two minutes."

The seven-year-old twins had been staying with their grandparents in England while he came to Norway ahead of them to get a house and wrap up his most pressing work project.

England held bittersweet memories, but Norway would be a fresh start for their little family of three. It might take a bit of time for the twins to learn the language and adjust to life in a different country, but it would be okay. They had Norwegian blood, after all.

Living here should come naturally, right?

He pulled into a driveway in a cul-de-sac. "Here we are."

As they got out of the car, he stole a glance at his mother-in-law's tight-lipped face. This modest bungalow didn't stand in comparison to Willowmere, the Georgian manor house in the Cotswolds that had been her daughter Charlotte's dream home.

But his late wife was gone now, and Chase and Mya's opinions were the only ones that mattered.

His son squirmed, catching Steinar's attention. "Dad, I need the toilet."

"I'll show you where it is." Steinar ushered them through the front door and pointed at the half bath just off the hallway. "Over there."

Mya followed Steinar into the living room, her blue gaze sweeping over the simple, practical decor. Shipping costs were exorbitant, so he'd not brought any of their furniture from England.

Since they were being forced to downsize, Steinar felt it would be much easier on the children to do it in a new country, where they wouldn't have to see constant reminders of the luxuries they could no longer afford.

Doris stood tight-lipped in the middle of the living room as she looked around her. "It's nice and snug."

Which was her way of saying tiny.

"Where's my room?" Mya asked.

"Over this way." Steinar led her down the hallway. "I thought you'd like this bedroom over here to the right."

Mya threw open the door and went into a room that wasn't much bigger than her old walk-in closet in Willowmere. Steinar had done his best, modeling the room after the girl's bedroom display in the IKEA catalog.

The walls were a pale gray backdrop to the powder pink high-sleeper bed and pink curtains. Steinar was especially proud of the flush mounted light, shaped like a pastel-colored rainbow and clouds.

Mya's face lit up. "That's so cool! And I like that high up bed. I've always wanted a bunk bed, but this is

the next best thing." She clambered up the ladder and perched on the foot of the bed.

Steinar breathed out his relief. Thank God she liked the space-saving bed and desk combo. He'd been worried she would miss her large princess canopy bed, but the ladder seemed to make up for the lack of posters and drapery. "You'll be able to do your homework on this desk under here."

Chase came down the hallway. "Ew, pink. Where's my room?"

"It's this one across from Mya's," Steinar said. "Have you washed your hands?"

The little boy spun around and returned to the bathroom.

"I want to put my things away," Mya said, glancing at the small wardrobe.

"I'll get your luggage from the car as soon as I've shown Chase his room."

"I wanna see Chase's room, too." Mya jumped down and scurried around Steinar. She stepped into the room across the hall, a twin version of hers, with its counterpart furniture in blues and grays. Instead of a rainbow and cloud, Chase's ceiling light was shaped like an airplane.

Chase walked toward them, water dripping from his hands. "Hey, no fair. You got to see my room before I did."

He flicked water droplets into Mya's face, making her squeal in annoyance.

Steinar pointed a warning finger at his son. "None of that, please. What do you think of your room?"

The boy shrugged. "It's nice, I guess. But where will I set up my train set?"

Steinar tried to keep his tone light. "I don't think there's room here to have your model railway the way it used to be. But it's tucked away safely, and perhaps someday we'll get the space to set it up again."

"Okay." Chase went off to examine the drawers under his high sleeper bed.

To Steinar's relief, the boy didn't look upset about his missing train set. It was packed away in storage in England, along with the bulk of the children's toys and clothes.

Chase and Mya had been forced to adjust to so many changes since their mother's passing two years ago. Everyone said children were resilient, like rubber. But even rubber had its breaking point. Steinar prayed he'd never find out what his children's breaking point was.

"I'll get your luggage from the car," he said, pausing as he came toward Doris, who stood in the hallway. "I'll set up an air mattress for you in Mya's room."

She nodded tersely. "I suppose I can cope with an air mattress for one night."

"I'm very grateful that you flew over with the children," he said. Steinar didn't see eye to eye with his mother-in-law on some things, but she was devoted to her grandchildren. It would have been impossible for him to fetch them from England himself and still meet his deadline.

The taut lines in her face relaxed. "You know I'd do anything to help. But I really wish they could have stayed longer. Didn't you say school isn't starting for another couple of weeks? If they'd stayed until after this weekend, they could have gone to the horse show. I don't suppose they have events like that here?"

"No," Steinar said tersely. He'd made the deliberate choice to get the children to Norway before the final equestrian event of the English summer. Although they'd been attending the Blatchery Palace Horse Trials since they were infants, they were no longer part of that horsey set. It would have been yet another reminder of the lifestyle his children had to leave behind. A lifestyle he could no longer afford.

His in-laws would have happily paid for the twins to continue with their expensive hobbies, plugging the gap between Steinar's current income and what he used to earn.

But Steinar didn't want his children to take for granted luxuries that were now outside his budget. Doris found it hard to understand why he resisted handouts. It was one of the areas of friction between them.

He could provide a modest lifestyle for them, and he wanted them to be content with that. If they wanted more, he was raising them to value the hard work and perseverance it would take to get those extras.

Steinar went to the car and came back with the first load of luggage.

Mya stood next to her grandmother in the living room. They were looking out the French windows, their backs facing Steinar.

"It's an okay house," Mya said. "The backyard looks pretty small, but I really like my bedroom."

Doris kissed the top of the little girl's head. "I'll miss you all. But, hopefully, we'll see you at Christmas."

Steinar put the suitcases down. "What was that about Christmas?"

"Oh, I just said to Mya that I might see you at Christmas." Doris turned to face him. "You'll be coming to spend the holidays with us, won't you?"

Steinar frowned. "I haven't made any plans yet." Even as he spoke, his gut resisted the idea of going back to England at Christmas. He and his children needed to build roots in their new home. How would Chase and Mya settle in Norway if they spent every holiday back in England?

Doris sounded put out. "Well, let me know soon so that we can plan accordingly." Her face brightened. "And Mya, your aunt Vivian said she wants to visit you sometime this autumn."

Steinar caught the sidelong glance Doris threw his way as Mya clapped and yelled, "Yay, Aunt Vivian!"

Steinar liked the idea of that visit from his sister-in-law even less than the thought of spending Christmas in England. But there was no polite way to object.

Sighing, he picked up Mya's suitcase and headed toward her room.

Chapter Three

AS SOON AS SHE got home, Reidun went straight into the bathroom to wash her hands. Towing a stranded vehicle wasn't the cleanest job.

She hoped Steinar and his family had reached home safely.

Hunger gnawed at her gut, but she knew she wouldn't find anything enticing in the fridge or cupboard.

Sure enough, her options were less than promising. Not even a TV dinner. A quick scan of the shelves revealed it would be another meal of microwaved

noodles. She poked the plastic film and set the timer.

Her best friend Johanna, shockingly, cooked for fun. Before Johanna got married a few months ago, Reidun used to drop into her house unannounced, able to count on a filling snack or a full-on meal. Johanna was always trying out a new recipe that she wanted a second opinion on.

It had been a while since they'd had a good, long chat. She picked up her phone, but the call went straight to voicemail. Strange, since Johanna lived with her phone in her hand. Reidun tried Bethany, another of her good friends. That went to voicemail, too, doubly weird. Why wasn't anyone answering their phones?

She pulled up another number. Sonia was usually good for a nice chat. She hit the call button, smiling as the call connected.

"Hello?" Sonia's voice was a low whisper.

"Hey, Sonia. What's up? Why are you talking like that?"

"Hang on." A few moments later, she spoke in her normal voice. "Sorry about that. I was in a meeting and everyone stared at me when my phone rang."

"What meeting? Something to do with the community center?"

"No, we're at the church married couples' retreat."

Reidun's face heated. "Oh. Was that this weekend?" No wonder she'd not

gotten through to Bethany or Johanna. They must be there, too, with their husbands.

Not too long ago, all of Reidun's closest friend group had been single. Now, four of them were newly married. Or, in the case of one of them, newly reconciled to a formerly estranged husband. Either way, her best friends were now all coupled up. It wasn't so simple anymore for them to have a girls' night out, or even a long one-on-one chat.

"I'm sorry for interrupting you," Reidun said.

"Was it anything urgent?"

Reidun shook her head. "No. Nothing urgent. I just wanted to chat. Get back to your meeting, and I'll catch up with you later."

She ended the call. Marriage retreat weekend? So, that meant another weekend when none of her friends would be available to hang out. Not that they'd been all that available lately, anyway. Quiet nights in like this were becoming Reidun's norm. She had some hobbies she enjoyed, like wood-turning, hiking, or painting, but she didn't want to do them all the time.

How sad was it that she knew exactly which shows were coming on TV every evening of the week? Tonight her choices lay between a police procedural, a family drama, and a reality dating show.

Or maybe she could start a new wood-turning project. Her gaze strayed toward the workshop where she kept her lathe. There was some salvaged hardwood she'd got from a construction site last month that might make some interesting chess pieces.

She sat up straight. She'd forgotten. There was an online orientation meeting tonight for vendors participating in the neighboring town's Christmas fair.

The wooden vases, bowls, and candlesticks she made as a hobby were popular gifts among her friends, and seven years ago she'd started selling them at the Christmas fair. It was a nice way to earn some extra cash and stop her projects from cluttering up her storage space.

The organizers of the Havdal Christmas fair hosted an online orientation meeting for all interested vendors just before applications opened. Like all the other vendors, Reidun had to apply for her spot at the fair every year. It was little more than a formality, but she liked to get her application in early. And attending the orientation meeting was something to do.

It was starting on Zoom in fifteen minutes, which gave her plenty of time to finish her noodles.

Reidun opened her email and clicked on the meeting link. The host let her in, and she debated whether to turn her camera on.

She ran a hand through her short hair. Ah, why not? It wasn't as though anyone else would look their best, anyway. She clicked on the gallery view of the meeting, checking out who else was attending.

From one window, an excited dog barked, followed by a yell of "Shut up!"

Reidun grinned. Someone always forgot to mute their microphone at these things. She double-checked hers just in case.

There were some names she recognized among the attendees. Since Berghaven didn't have a Christmas fair of its own, several vendors like herself plied their wares at Havdal's event. Some, like her, did it as a hobby or for side income, but there were a few charity groups who used the event to raise funds, and some small businesses for whom the Christmas fair was a key part of their annual income.

One of Havdal's municipal councilors began the meeting, smoothing his slicked back black hair as he spoke. "Thanks for attending and showing your interest in participating in this year's Christmas fair in Havdal. Your participation has made this event a success for the past twenty-five years. We have some exciting developments to announce. This year, we're going to be even more eco-friendly. We'll cut down on single use items, have more recycling stations, and prioritize reusable materials where possible. We are also developing a mobile app and website that will give real-time information, interactive maps, and updates."

Reidun tapped her fingers on her desk as he went through his list of improvements. That all sounded good. When would he share the sign-up link, though?

After speaking for several more minutes, the meeting chairman cleared his throat. "With all these improvements, we've had to update our pricing structure for vendor fees. Full details are on our sign-up page, but given the success and growth of Havdal's fair, we're increasing our rates to be more in line with comparable fees in towns similar to ours. The link should be available in the chat window, if the technical team has put it there."

Finally, the sign-up page. Reidun found the link and clicked on it. She scanned the verbiage while listening to the chairman droning on.

Her gaze skipped down to the fee amount and the link to pay and secure her spot. What was this? That couldn't be right. The fee amount was over three times what she'd paid last year. Was there some kind of mistake?

She read the page more carefully. As always, vendors from outside Havdal were being charged a higher rate. That was understandable, since the town had to support its own local business community. But from what she could tell, the local vendor pricing had only gone up a little, while non-locals like her were being asked to pay three times last year's fees.

She left her browser and clicked back into Zoom. The meeting chat was blowing up, with every comment about the vendor fees. But not everyone was as indignant as she was. It was smart of the organizers to make sure their new pricing structure only hammered vendors from outside Havdal. Divide and conquer.

She hoped the chairman was going to open this up for questions, because she had a few. It was going to be impossible for her to make a profit with such an increase in vendor fees, not including the money it would already cost her to travel to Havdal and set up an attractive display.

She tuned in to the chairman, who was speaking once again.

"I can see some comments coming through now, and most of them are about the new fee structure. Our costs reflect the expansion in our services and recognition that the Havdal Christmas fair is the premier holiday event in the region. We're confident that vendors with high-quality offerings will make their money back, despite the higher fees."

Reidun clicked on the chat window to enter her own comment, her fingers flying over the keyboard.

Isn't tripling the vendor price for non-local businesses extreme? It's

understandable that we have to pay for new services and features, but this is disproportionately hard on vendors who come from outside Havdal.

She drummed her fingers on the table as she waited for the meeting chairman to acknowledge her comment. It was soon buried by a flood of others who were in support of the new fee structure. They must all be based in Havdal, relieved that outsiders were carrying the cost of the new facilities they were all going to enjoy.

This was beyond infuriating. Wasn't the chairman going to acknowledge her comment?

Her phone rang. It was Diane, a fellow vendor at the Christmas fair. Reidun had seen her among the meeting attendees. "Hi, Diane."

"Hi, Reidun. I saw you on this Zoom call. Can you believe what they're trying to pull?"

"I know, right?"

"It's going to wipe out most of my profits. I can't afford to pay this," Diane said.

Reidun caught the tremble in the other woman's voice. Diane topped up her state pension with her handmade soap and candles. While the Havdal Christmas Fair was a nice bit of extra income for Reidun, it was what enabled Diane to get Christmas and

birthday presents for her grandchildren.

A thought struck her. About half of the vendors came from Berghaven. Why did they have to enrich Havdal's coffers? Weren't there enough of them to set up their own Christmas fair?

She voiced the thought aloud to Diane. "Why doesn't Berghaven have its own Christmas fair?" She'd lived in the town her whole life, and for as long as she could remember, the big Christmas event was the fair held in the neighboring town. Things had always been that way. But did they have to stay that way?

"How would that work?" Diane asked. "Who would even organize it?"

"The Chamber of Commerce, maybe?"

"I'm not a member. Are you?"

"Yes," Reidun said slowly. Although it had been months since she'd last attended a meeting. "There's a chamber of commerce meeting next week. I'm going to bring it up. I'm sure they'll be equally outraged about what Havdal is trying to do, especially since they're supposed to stand up for the interests of local business people in Berghaven, right?"

"Okay. Well, good luck. Let me know how it goes. The worst they can say is no, right?"

"Right." Reidun ended the call.

She turned back to her laptop screen. The chairman was winding up

the meeting now, without ever ad-dressing her question, never mind the dozens of other vendors who were equally upset about the price hike.

She clicked the window shut. It was definitely time Berghaven had a Christmas fair of its own.

Chapter Four

WERE THERE ANY PEOPLE who actually enjoyed networking?

Reidun hovered at the edges of a knot of people who surrounded Oskar Nyland, chairman of Berghaven's Chamber of Commerce.

The chamber held these business breakfast events every month to help local entrepreneurs get to know each other and build connections, but Reidun would much rather be fitting a boiler than making small talk.

She was already busy enough at work that she didn't need to schmooze in order to get new clients. And she wasn't here today to drum up business. She was here to test the waters about the chamber backing a Christmas fair in Berghaven. Schmoozing would, unfortunately, be required. And it wasn't going well.

The dress code was business casual but, judging from what the other women were wearing, she was leaning too far toward the "casual" end of the description. Her khaki cargo pants and chunky black loafers stood out among the pencil skirts and kitten heels. It was like being in high school again and turning up in the wrong outfit.

She hoped to have a word with Oskar, but it was mortifying to be among one of the eager hangers-on hoping for a chance to speak to him. His blue-eyed gaze locked briefly with hers, flickered over her attire, and slid away again.

Reidun's face burned. Why did she have to deal with him? The events of twenty-five years ago were water under the bridge, and she'd learned to co-exist with him in this small town, although she didn't enjoy interacting with him. But if she was going to sell the idea of Berghaven having its own Christmas fair, she'd need his support in one way or another.

She blinked as she recognized Steinar, the handsome guy she'd

pulled out of the ditch a few days ago. So, he was a member of the Chamber of Commerce. Interesting. And apparently on excellent terms with Oskar, judging from the way they were smiling and talking. What was his line of business?

She had to stay on task right now, though, not speculate about good-looking guys. After this informal networking session, everyone would sit down to breakfast at randomly assigned tables, where they'd network some more.

Following that would be a session where Oskar would make some remarks and take questions. But it would be easiest to talk to him now. She hated public speaking and wanted to avoid speaking in front of the entire meeting, if she could.

Reidun sidled closer to the center of the group around the chairman and waited for an opening in the conversation. Finally, a tiny lull. Stepping forward, Reidun pounced on the opportunity to speak to Oskar. "Have you heard—"

A ripple of chimes burst through the sound system, followed by the master of ceremonies' mellow voice. "Ladies and gentlemen, we hope you've enjoyed your opportunity to mingle with some of the other guests. I'm informed that breakfast is served, so would you please make your way to your assigned tables? Your table number should be printed on your name tag."

Reidun balled her fists in frustration. Why did the MC have to interrupt right when she'd finally got the chance to talk to Oskar? Now she'd have to either buttonhole him later on or raise her question in the membership meeting after breakfast. In front of everyone. She hoped she could avoid that.

She glanced at her tag. Table three. She took her seat near the side of the room. Her breakfast companions were a real estate agent, the owner of a fish canning firm, and one of the partners in an accounting firm.

The real estate agent's eyes brightened when Reidun sat down. "Miss

Norberg of Norberg Plumbing Solutions, right?"

"That's right."

"Karl Hagen of Hagen Realty." He held out his hand. "I've been planning on getting in touch with you for a while, so this is serendipity."

She returned his handshake. "Really? What an interesting coincidence."

He launched into a long explanation about some property management contract his firm had just gained. "Our client wants to rent the apartments out to students. The plumbing needs some serious updating and the volume of work is beyond what our normal partners can cope with. So, we thought of you."

He continued to talk eagerly about his new property and its plumbing needs.

A waiter came to her elbow with a coffee refill. Several other waiters cleared away the plates. Was breakfast already over? She'd been so engrossed in explaining to Karl the advantages of a heat pump over a furnace system that she hadn't had time for more than a couple of bites of bacon and scrambled eggs.

The MC spoke into the microphone, bringing the hum of talk to a stop. "I hope you're all enjoying this delicious breakfast. Time is moving along, so we're going to go into the next session. I'll invite our executive secretary to give us some announcements, after which our chairman will share some remarks."

When the updates were over, Oskar stepped onto the stage. "It's time to open the floor up to questions. As you know, it's my firm belief that this is your chamber of commerce. Your concerns are our concerns, and we can build Berghaven together. My only request is that all comments be limited to two minutes so that we use the time most effectively. And with that, fire away. Your board is listening."

Sweat made Reidun's palms slick. She wanted to give up the idea of saying anything, but she couldn't. Diane and the other vendors were counting on her to at least try to find out whether the chamber would support a Christmas fair.

She pushed her hand into the air before she could talk herself out of it.

Reidun's tongue clung to the roof of her mouth as she stood up. Everyone was looking at her. Heat crawled up her neck.

"I, um... I wanted to ask a question about the Christmas fair. Because it's something that a lot of us participate in and sell our products, but in Havdal." She swallowed, in an effort to give moisture to her cottony mouth. "I... That is, some of us thought it might be something to consider doing in Berghaven. The vendor fees have become so high now that it's hard to keep doing it especially for those who want to make it profitable. So, is it something the chamber of commerce might want to support?"

Her face flaming, she sank back into her seat. Had anyone even deciphered her point after that rambling, stammering, jumble of words?

Oskar smiled. "Thank you for your contribution, Miss Norberg. Some interesting thoughts there. Moving on, the floor is still open. Yes, Mr. Hansen."

Mr. Hansen spoke at length about parking regulations and how unfair parking fines were throttling business in the town center.

Another speaker wanted to talk about how the chamber might collaborate with the local high school about workplace development programs. Reidun might have found his question interesting if she hadn't been squirming over how her own comment had sunk like a lead balloon.

So, that was it. Diane and the others would have to suck up Havdal's exorbitant new fees, or not participate in any Christmas market at all.

Oskar spoke to the next speaker. "Yes, Mr. Jakobsen. What do you have to say?"

"Thanks. I want to follow up on a comment that was made earlier, which I feel we need to explore more. The lady who spoke, Miss Norberg, I think, asked about why Berghaven doesn't have a Christmas fair, given all the benefits it might bring to the town."

Reidun looked up at the sound of her name, and her heart lurched. It was Steinar, the man from the ditch, who was speaking.

He stood with his hands resting lightly on his hips, oozing confidence. "If I understood her correctly, she said there are a good number of vendors from this town who have been helping to make the Havdal Christmas market a success. I'm sure there are good reasons why Berghaven has chosen not to have its own fair in the past, but I'm curious about whether those reasons still exist."

As Steinar spoke, Reidun's pulse thundered in her ears. She glanced at Oskar's face. The man was giving Steinar his full attention.

Oskar nodded his head. "Thanks for your intervention, Steinar. You've raised some good points. Mikkel, I see your hand. Let's hear your comment."

Reidun turned her attention to the next speaker. She couldn't remember his surname, but he ran a bed and breakfast. "I just wanted to say that Steinar's question is a good one. I've often wondered why we send so much business Havdal's way yet we could get the same benefits. Every year, without fail, I've had guests who ask about seasonal events in December, and I've had to direct them over to the

Havdal Christmas market. Why shouldn't they spend their shopping money here?"

Oskar rubbed his chin. "Okay," he said slowly. "I can see this issue has garnered a lot of interest. Let's do this. Steinar, I'm nominating you to lead a sub-committee to explore the possibility of Berghaven hosting a Christmas fair. You'll need to present a feasibility report to the executive committee. Are you up for it?"

Steinar's eyebrows flew up. "Me? Okay, sure, I'm happy to help."

"Excellent. I'll send your terms of reference via email." Oskar looked toward Reidun. "And since she brought up the idea, I'd also like to nominate

Miss Norberg to serve on the sub-committee, if she's willing."

Unable to trust her voice, Reidun answered Oskar with a nod.

"Excellent," Oskar said. "Liaise with Steinar about your next steps. We're out of time, so I'll hand the floor back to our MC."

Reidun sat quietly as the MC's voice went on. They were going to at least explore the idea of Berghaven having a fair. Thank God Steinar had backed up her shambolic display. Otherwise they would probably have dismissed her completely.

Chapter Five

STEINAR WEAVED HIS WAY past the people milling about the dining hall. His Good Samaritan towing plumber was hard to miss, not just because of her statuesque figure, but because she was one of the few women here.

She stood near a window, slightly apart from the crowd, one hand clutching the strap of her purse. As he approached her, her gaze swiveled to meet his.

Now that she wasn't wearing a raincoat with the hood pulled down, he had his first proper look at her eyes. They were exquisite. A deep luscious brown, they tilted upward at the corners.

And they were almost level with his. He rarely met such tall women. His own Charlotte had barely come up to his shoulder.

He held out his hand. "I'm Steinar Jakobsen. First of all, I didn't even thank you properly for helping us out the other day."

The grip of her long, slender fingers was strong. Very strong.

"Reidun Norberg. You're welcome. Like I said, anyone else in town would have stopped to help."

"I appreciate it, nonetheless. Well, Reidun, it looks like we've both been tapped to figure out this Christmas fair thing. Great idea, by the way."

She inclined her head. "Thanks. It only seemed to get traction after you spoke up. I'm surprised you even understood what I was trying to say. Could I have been any more incoherent?"

She chuckled, so he smiled back.

A thought struck him that wiped away his smile. "Does it bother you that I was asked to head this sub-committee? Because I honestly don't mind stepping aside. It was your idea, after all."

She stared at him for a moment, then shook her head. "To be honest, it did grind my gears. But only for half a second. When you're the only female plumber in town, it gets exhausting having to fight to be heard. But then again, I botched my pitch and you got them to actually listen. So, as far as I'm concerned, none of that matters. The important thing is that we do our best to make this thing happen."

He nodded. "What gave you the idea for Berghaven to have a Christmas fair?"

"I've been taking part in the Havdal fair for a few years now. I sell handmade wooden bowls and things like that. But this year, they're charging three times the normal vendor fee. And the higher fee only applies to vendors coming from outside Havdal. And so I thought, we have so much talent and high-quality products made in our own town. Why can't we have our own Christmas fair?" Her face grew more animated, and she gestured with her hands. "Couldn't Berghaven's business community capture some of that foot traffic and revenue that's been making its way to Havdal all these years? Their Christmas fair is a huge tourist attraction, and I think we're leaving money on the table by not having something of our own."

She was very articulate when she got excited. He looked at her for a moment. "You really want this Christmas fair to happen, don't you?"

"Don't you?"

He paused for a moment, considering her question. The thought of a

Christmas fair hadn't crossed his mind until about half an hour ago. He'd only become intrigued by the idea when he recognized her as she stood up to propose it. Then he'd given the thing a nudge when it appeared it had been lost in the shuffle.

He shrugged. "I guess it would be nice, but I'm here with an open mind. We're supposed to scope out whether it's feasible or not. And since I'm a newcomer, I have no preconceived ideas."

"So, what brought you over to Berghaven?"

Steinar had his packaged answer ready. "I grew up in West Finnmark but I've been living in England for the past twenty years. My children and I needed a new start, so we moved over here."

"That explains why your wife and children were speaking English."

What was she talking about? "My wife?"

Reidun gave him a double take. "The lady in the car with you the other day. Wasn't she—"

"Oh." He laughed. "That was my mother-in-law. My wife was a good deal younger than me, and there aren't many years between me and Doris. My wife passed away."

She ducked her head. "Oh. I'm sorry for your loss."

"Thank you."

There was a pause. Steinar spoke first. "So, how shall we go about doing this feasibility study?"

She pulled out her phone. "We should probably decide when to meet. The sooner the better."

"Sure." He followed suit and got his phone out. "How about Wednesday? I'm flexible about the time."

"Sounds good. I'm free in the afternoon, from five o'clock onwards. Where should we meet?"

He typed the appointment into his phone and glanced up at her. "You're more familiar with this town than I am. Any suggestions?"

"There's a nice café at the Berghaven Mall. It's central and easy to get to. Shall we meet there at five?"

"Sounds good. See you on Wednesday."

His gaze followed her as she walked away. Reidun Norberg interested him a lot. He was looking forward to meeting her again.

Chapter Six

REIDUN READ HER DOCUMENT yet again, scrutinizing every word she'd written.

She'd sounded like an incoherent babbler last time she tried to sell the idea of a Christmas fair to Berghaven's chamber of commerce. This time, she wanted her ideas to sound clear and well thought out.

In under an hour, she would meet Steinar to work on a feasibility report for Oskar and his executive board.

This document contained her ideas towards the report.

She glanced at her watch. She was planning on walking to the café, so she'd better print this out now and leave.

Her phone rang as she retrieved the printout from her printer.

"Hello, Steinar" she said.

"Hi. I'm really sorry, but my babysitter has just canceled on me."

"Sorry to hear that. Do you need to reschedule our meeting?"

"No, I want to go ahead with it. But since I'll have my children with me, perhaps the café isn't the best venue. If you don't mind, could we meet at my place? It'll be easier to keep them occupied here. We live out near the harbor."

Reidun's heart sank. "That would have been okay, but I don't have a vehicle today. My truck's timing belt broke this afternoon, so it's in the garage for repairs. I was planning to go to the café on foot, but your place is a bit too far for me to walk. Or, at least, not if we want the meeting to start at six."

"I see. Do you want to postpone, then?"

Reidun hesitated. The sooner they got the ball rolling on this Christmas fair thing, the better. It had been tricky enough to find a time that worked for both of them. "Why don't you bring the children here? I can put on cartoons or something to keep them busy while we talk."

"Are you sure?"

No, she wasn't. "Um... It's fine. Just come along. I'll text you my address."

"Thanks. See you soon."

Reidun ended the call. She couldn't remember the last time she'd had children in her home. But Steinar's twins weren't babies, so she presumably didn't need to worry about childproofing, right?

Would they expect a snack or a drink? Hopefully not, because the only drink she had was sparkling water. And she wasn't sure they'd like any of the food she had on hand.

But this meeting shouldn't take long. She grabbed her printout and gave it a last look over.

Her heart thudded when the doorbell rang, and she chided herself for being so silly.

Steinar's huge frame filled her doorway, and Mya and Chase stood in front of him, staring up at her with wide blue eyes. They really were exceptionally beautiful children, like the models in a catalog for a high-end clothes store.

"Hi," she said. "Come in."

She stepped back as the Jakobsens crowded her hallway. "You can just leave your boots and shoes at the door, and put your coats on the coat rack over there."

Reidun hovered nearby, watching as Steinar took his children's coats.

He slid off his jacket. "Thanks for having us at such short notice."

"No problem." She switched to English. "Children, if you'll come over here, I'll put something on for you to watch on the TV."

They followed her into the living room and settled onto the sofa, their feet dangling above the floor.

Chase pointed toward the TV table. "You have a Nintendo Switch?"

"Yes, I do."

"What games have you got?"

"Let's see." She knelt next to the TV table and slid open the cabinet door. "I have these ones over here, plus a few more that are digital downloads."

Both children jumped off the sofa. Crouched next to her, they scanned her game collection.

Chase gasped. "You've got *The Legend of Zelda: Breath of the Wild*? And *Tears of the Kingdom*, too?" He picked up one of the game boxes.

"Yes. I'm a huge Zelda fan. Have you played them?"

Chase glanced at Steinar. "No. Not these ones. Dad says I have to wait until I'm eight. But I've played some other Zelda games."

"You have? Which ones?"

"*Skyward Sword* and *Windwaker*."

"Oh, I love those," Reidun said. "I've got them both, but it's been a while since I played them."

Chase sat back on his heels. "My friend Giles in England has beaten *Breath of the Wild* in Master Mode."

Reidun grinned. "So have I. One hundred percented it, in fact."

"Really?" Chase's eyes grew round. "Did you complete the Trial of the Sword and the Champions' Ballad?"

"I did."

He narrowed his eyes. "What about the korok seeds?"

"I found all nine hundred and ninety-nine."

Reidun could see her stock rising in the little boy's eyes as his jaw fell open. It felt surprisingly gratifying to impress a seven-year-old.

She turned to Mya. "Do you like video games, too?"

Mya nodded. "I play *Pokémon*. And *MarioKart*."

"I've actually got *MarioKart* as a digital download. Do you want to play that now instead of watching TV?"

Both children turned toward their father. "Can we?" Chase asked.

"Yes, of course," Steinar said. "But no arguing if you lose."

Reidun set up the play environment, then faced Steinar. "Perhaps we could work over here on the dining table?"

She gestured toward a chair, and Steinar took a seat.

He glanced at his children, who were engrossed in their game. "That's their absolute favorite thing to do together, so they should be happy for a while. I thought we could begin by putting our heads together and brainstorming some of the issues and roadblocks we'll need to research about running a Christmas fair. And then we can see what we need to find out and take it from there."

"Actually, I already made a start." Reidun pulled out the document she'd printed out. "I outlined the steps we need to take to organize a Christmas fair in this town, and identified the groups we'd need to involve."

"You did? Let's have a look." He pulled the printed pieces of paper toward himself and scanned the document. "Potential obstacles, budgetary limitations, weather concerns, a need for volunteers, getting planning permission..."

He read quietly for a moment longer, then looked up at Reidun. "These are all good points, and I like that you've also mentioned how we can get over each of these hurdles. This should go a long way toward making that feasibility report."

She liked the fact that he'd said "we."

"Dad, I'm hungry." Chase's voice came from the sofa.

Reidun cringed. This was exactly what she'd been dreading. She hadn't planned on giving her guests any refreshments.

Steinar looked at his son, his face reddening. "We'll get something to eat as soon as we're done here. We won't be long."

"But I'm hungry now."

Steinar sighed, turning to Reidun. "I'm sorry. The babysitter was going to get them dinner, and I completely forgot."

Reidun bit her lip. What on earth would she serve them? "I've got *knekkebrød* and cheese. Could they have that while we finish off?"

Steinar frowned. "They've never tried *knekkebrød*, but thanks. I really appreciate that."

Reidun went to her kitchen and pulled out a packet of the crispbread made with wholemeal rye flour that was a staple in many Norwegian homes. She spread a few pieces with butter and cheese and took the plates out to the children, along with glasses of water.

Chase eyed his plate as though it would bite him.

"What's that?" Mya asked.

"It's *knekkebrød* with cheese. It tastes a bit like crackers or toast."

The boy nibbled on a corner of the rectangular piece of crispbread, then took a large bite.

Mya watched her brother's reaction, then bit into hers. Her eyes widened as she chewed. "It's yummy."

Reidun blew out a sigh of relief. "I'm really glad you like it. Let me know if you want any more."

She went back to the dining table, where Steinar sat watching his children, a smile on his face.

He leaned forward and spoke quietly. "They're very picky eaters, and I have the hardest time getting them to try anything new. Thank you."

A thought suddenly struck her. "I didn't offer you anything. Are you hungry? Can I get you a cup of coffee?"

"Since you're offering, I'd really like a bit of *knekkebrød*, too, please."

"I'll get it while you read the rest of that." She gestured toward the papers he still held.

She fixed his snack and got two mugs of coffee ready, taking them to the table as he turned over the last page.

He looked up at her. "Thanks. This is an excellent piece of work. I think you've touched on all the relevant questions the executive committee will have, and this makes a powerful case for Berghaven to host its own Christmas fair."

Her heart glowed. "You think so?"

"I do. You've pretty much written the feasibility report, so all that's left for me to do is email it to Oskar. I've got a really good feeling about this. I think the other members of the board will see it the same way."

A loud crash rang out just as Steinar finished speaking.

Reidun jumped, spinning toward the living room.

Mya stood red-faced, pieces of shattered glass around her feet, mixed in with a pool of water.

Reidun rushed toward the child. "Did you hurt yourself?"

Mya shook her head.

"Good. That's the most important thing. Now, stand well back so you don't step into any of this glass, okay?"

Steinar came toward the sofa. "What happened?"

"She dropped her glass," Chase said.

"I didn't do it on purpose." Tears filled Mya's eyes.

"Of course you didn't," Reidun said. "One glass? That's nothing. I broke two plates just the other day."

Steinar reached out and lifted the little girl. "Come on, Chase, let's step clear of this mess."

Mya buried her face into her father's shoulder and he grazed the top of her head with his lips.

Steinar turned to Reidun. "I'm really sorry about this."

"It's not a big deal at all. Accidents happen."

He stroked Mya's hair, then set the girl back on her feet. "I think it'd be a good time for us to go. Thanks for all the work you did. If you could send it to me by email, I'll forward it to Oskar."

Reidun nodded. "I don't think I have your email address."

"I'll text it to you. Come on, children. What do you say?"

Chase and Mya spoke in chorus. "Thanks, Reidun."

"You're welcome."

She followed them to the door and watched as they got their shoes and coats on.

Steinar faced her. "I'm glad about how things went. I have a good feeling about this."

She smiled back. She did, too.

Chapter Seven

As Reidun walked across the church parking lot on Sunday, she did a double take. Was that Steinar and his children?

She quickened her steps. It was them.

He turned toward her as she came up to them, his eyebrows rising high above his widening eyes. "Hello, Reidun. You come to this church?"

"I do. Hi, children."

"Hi," they answered in chorus.

She faced Steinar again. "So, you're a church family? I've been a member of Bethel Church since I was in my teens."

"We've been trying to find a church home, so we've done the rounds. We went to St. Olavs for a couple of weeks, then we checked out Berghaven Christian Center last week, and today we're visiting."

"Well, I'm obviously biased, but I hope you'll like this place." She glanced at the children. "Most of the teaching is in Norwegian, but we're used to guests from other countries."

"That sounds good," Steinar said.

She fell into step beside him as they headed toward the door. "Have you

heard anything about the Christmas fair yet?"

He shook his head. "I added a few small tweaks to the document you wrote, and sent it to Oskar. He confirmed he'd received my email, but since then there's been nothing but crickets."

Reidun frowned. That was over two weeks ago. What could be holding things up? "If they take too long to move on this, we may not have time to organize a Christmas fair for this year."

"I'm actually having lunch with Oskar and his family today. Just after this service, in fact. I'll give him a nudge to find out what's going on."

Steinar was chummy enough with Oskar to be going over for lunch? That made Reidun uneasy. Aloud, she said, "That's a good idea."

They got to the door where Reidun's friends, Sonia and Axel Vikhammer, were on greeting duty today.

Sonia's smile broadened as she glanced from Steinar to Reidun. "Morning, Reidun. Have you brought a friend today?"

Reidun's face heated. "This is Steinar Jakobsen and his children, Mya and Chase. They've just moved to Berghaven from England."

She switched to English and spoke to the children. "Mya, Chase, this is my really good friend, Sonia. And this is her husband Axel. You'll have to excuse him, because he tells the world's worst jokes."

Axel grinned, speaking to the children in heavily accented English. "Only because I learn them all from Reidun. Welcome to Berghaven, and welcome to Bethel Church."

As they headed for the sanctuary, Reidun caught the curious glances from the church members they passed. If she sat with Steinar and the children during the service, people might draw all manner of conclusions.

She blew out a relieved sigh as Ingrid, the pastor's wife, came bustling over. Reidun could hand Steinar and the children off to her.

Ingrid's smile was warm and welcoming. "Good morning! Welcome to

Bethel Church. Friends of yours, Reidun?"

Reidun made the introductions, then slipped away, grinning to herself as Ingrid took the Jakobsens under her wing. The pastor's wife's English was rudimentary, but that didn't dim her enthusiastic chatter with the children.

Reidun moved to her usual seat a few rows back and kept an eye on them throughout the service.

Steinar sang along with all the songs. The children spent most of the time with their markers and coloring books.

After the service, she hung back as several other church members gathered around the Jakobsens. It was good to see them being so warmly welcomed, and she hoped they'd stay.

Bethel Church was a wonderful place for families and couples. Throughout the year, there were programs, courses, and all sorts of events about strengthening bonds and building discipleship within the home. Engaged couples had a lot of robust resources, too. Singles, though, were pretty much on their own. Literally.

Until a few months ago, Reidun and her best single friends had a tradition of a Sunday afternoon hike on one of the trails that went around Berghaven. But, one by one, the friends had gotten married and naturally wanted to spend Sunday afternoons with their husbands and families. Sonia had brought her husband along once, but the dynamic just wasn't the same, so both she and he never came again.

The Sunday hike was a stark reminder of her solitude, so Reidun had stopped going.

Sometimes her friends asked her to join them for Sunday lunch, which was wonderful. She didn't do the same, though, because her cooking was abysmal.

She headed toward her car. Maybe she'd make those chess pieces. Or play a video game.

Hopefully, when Steinar had lunch with Oskar, he'd find out what was happening with the feasibility report and let her know.

Chapter Eight

STEINAR PULLED HIS CAR up to Oskar Nyland's home. He and Oskar had interacted at a handful of business events, and Steinar liked the man's sharp mind and confident demeanor. And since Steinar hoped to grow his client base among the business community here, Oskar was a good person to know.

The large house, with its immaculately presented front lawn, looked like exactly the kind of impressive home in which the chairman of the chamber of commerce would live.

Steinar activated the parking brake and twisted around to look at his children in the back seat. "Okay, guys, we're here. The Nylands have kindly invited us for lunch. That means they've taken the trouble to get things ready for us, and they're offering us food they hope we'll find really delicious. Remember how we behave when we're asked out for a meal?"

"Yes, Dad," the twins replied in chorus.

"Tell me so I can be sure."

Mya spoke up. "We say please and thank you, and if there's something we don't like, we say no thank you."

"Correct. And what else?"

"No making faces or gagging noises if we don't like the food," Chase said.

Crossing her arms, Mya glared at her brother. "You're the only one who does that."

"But at least I don't cry if there's any other flavor than vanilla ice cream."

"Enough, you two," Steinar said. "And have you got the flowers for Mrs. Nyland? Good. Let's go in."

Oskar welcomed them at the door with a wide smile. "Good to see you all. Please come in."

His wife Elsa walked into the hall-way, a frilly apron over her dress. Her stunning, dark-haired beauty was the perfect counterpart to Oskar's fair looks.

Although there was no physical re-semblance, something about Elsa reminded Steinar of his own late wife.

Perhaps it was the combination of elegant poise with stylish domesticity. Like Charlotte, she appeared to be a woman who could make a three course meal for a family of eight without breaking a sweat, and look good doing it.

Chase stepped forward, delivering the bouquet of flowers with a bow of his head. "These are for you, Mrs. Nyland. Thanks for having us over today."

Steinar suppressed a grin. His son could really lay on the charm when he wanted to.

Elsa took the flowers, one manicured hand pressed on her chest. "What a perfect little gentleman! Thank you so much. It's no trouble at

all to have you. Please come through this way."

They followed her into a large, bright living room. She turned to face the children. "We just got the most beautiful betta fish for our aquarium. Do you want to have a look?"

The children's faces lit up as they followed Elsa.

Left alone with Oskar, Steinar decided to grab the moment and get the question of the Christmas fair out of the way. "Any further thoughts about that feasibility study I emailed you?"

Oskar's jaw stiffened, but he soon masked it with a smile. "Yes, I've read it, and it's a very well put together document. It covers all the ground I expected, and more."

"I have to give credit where it's due," Steinar said. "Reidun wrote ninety-nine percent of it, and all I did was top and tail it before I forwarded it to you."

"Oh, did she?" Oskar asked. He walked over to a tray of drinks on the sideboard. "Would you like something to drink?"

"An orange juice would be nice, thanks." Steinar couldn't read his friend's expression.

Oskar handed him a glass filled with juice and tinkling ice. "How do you find working with Reidun?"

"It's been fine so far," Steinar said. "We've only had the one working session, but she's smart, focused, and great at taking the initiative."

A smile twisted Oskar's lips. "Some might refer to that as bossiness."

"I didn't get that impression at all," Steinar said.

"Reidun and I go back a very long way." Oskar glanced at Steinar over the rim of his glass. "In fact, if things had gone a bit differently, she would have been here instead of Elsa."

Steinar almost dropped his glass. "You and Reidun used to date?"

"More than that. We were weeks away from getting married."

Steinar stared at him. He couldn't imagine a universe where Reidun and Oskar were romantically involved, much less about to get married. "What happened?"

"I realized that I was making a big mistake. Not that there's anything wrong with Reidun—she was a very nice girl. She probably still is. But deep down, I knew we weren't suited for each other. Our lives were going in very different directions and I needed a wife who would support me while I pursued my dreams. I knew that my chosen career was going to be very demanding, and I had to have a wife who understood that. Reidun, lovely as she was, wasn't going to make those kinds of sacrifices."

"I see."

Oskar raised an eyebrow. "You know what I mean. From what I understand about your own career path, you couldn't have done what you did

without a wife who backed you one hundred percent."

Steinar nodded slowly. That was true. Charlotte was a stay-at-home wife long before they'd had children. She'd taken care of everything at home so he could put all his focus on building his business.

But why was Oskar even bringing this up? It seemed almost as though the man was trying to warn him off Reidun. Steinar wasn't even considering getting involved with her. All they had done was collaborate on a report for the chamber of commerce.

Oskar sipped his drink. "Breaking up with Reidun was a hard decision, especially since the wedding was only weeks away and the invitations had been sent out. And you know what it's like in a small town. People talk and take sides. Since you know both of us, I thought it was important to let you know."

Taking sides was one thing Steinar did not want to do. He'd heard enough. If Oskar told him any more, it was going to be weird interacting with Reidun. And he needed to work with her to see this project through.

He put his glass on the table. "Fair enough. But about the feasibility report. What did you think about the content? I think a Christmas fair would be a great thing for Berghaven. And the report shows we could pull it off with a bit of elbow grease."

Oskar turned his glass in his hands. "I agree that, on paper, it looks like a Christmas fair would be a good thing."

"Only on paper?"

Oskar sighed. "There are a lot of other things going on, Steinar. Having a Christmas fair in Berghaven looks like a good idea, but I have concerns about how it might come across to Havdal."

"What does Havdal have to do with it? It's a completely different town, and I wasn't aware we needed their permission to do things here."

"It's a different town, but we have a lot of common interests. I'm concerned that setting up a fair might seem like we're trying to take business from them. We risk antagonizing some influential businesses and individuals."

Steinar frowned. "By having a fair in a town forty-five minutes away? Perhaps it's because I'm a newcomer, but I honestly don't see it."

Oskar shot him a hard look. "Then you'll just have to trust my judgment. I've been involved in local politics and the business community most of my life. Sometimes we send business their way, and they send business our way. The Havdal Christmas fair is the biggest and most prominent seasonal event in this part of the country. It might be risky to go head-to-head."

"Does the rest of the executive committee agree with you?" Steinar asked.

Oskar broke eye contact. "They haven't seen the report yet."

Just then, Elsa came back into the room with Steinar's very excited children. Chase and Mya spoke over each other.

"Elsa let us feed the fish and they made my finger tickle."

"They're so pretty! Dad, can we get fish, too?"

Steinar laughed. "One at a time, please. We'll have to think about the fish. It's an enormous commitment."

Elsa hustled the children into the dining room for the meal, and Oskar went to the kitchen to help ferry things to the table.

Steinar wasn't satisfied with how their conversation had ended. But perhaps it was better he let the matter rest. He hoped Oskar didn't sit on the report too long, though, or it might indeed become too late to organize a Christmas fair this year.

Chapter Nine

REIDUN STARED AT THE agenda for the monthly meeting of Berghaven's chamber of commerce. She turned the paper over, then over again, rereading the printed words. There was no mention anywhere of the Christmas fair.

She looked around her, scouring the meeting hall for a glimpse of Steinar. She'd not seen him over the last couple of weeks beyond the occasional sighting across the room at church. She'd assumed that no news meant good news, and all was well.

But the fact that the fair was nowhere on the agenda didn't bode well. It would be another full month until the next meeting of the chamber of commerce. That would be in October, far too late to organize the event in time for this year's Christmas shopping season.

What had happened?

Oskar stood at the front of the room, looking his usual cool, self-assured self. He called the meeting to order, steering the discussion through each item of the agenda.

One by one, the discussion dealt with each item of business. Reidun stared at the last item: "AOB" or "any other business." This was when mem-

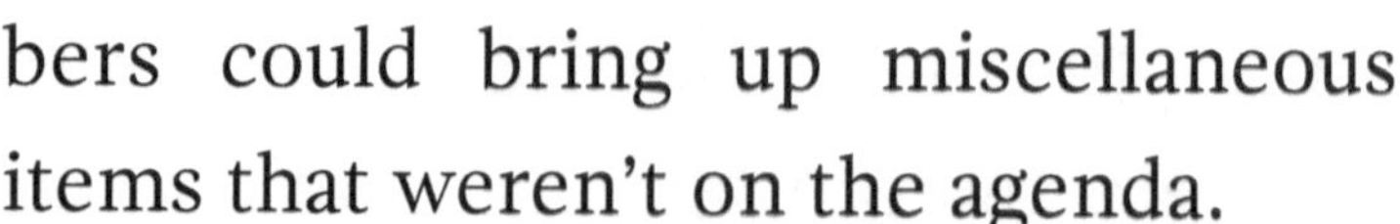

bers could bring up miscellaneous items that weren't on the agenda.

She could use that slot to raise her hand and ask what had happened since the executive committee had received the feasibility report, and what decision they'd made on whether to organize a Christmas fair.

But the last time she'd spoken to this group, she'd been a tongue-tied mess. The thought of speaking again made her stomach churn.

Oskar cleared his throat. "Let's move to the last item on the agenda. Is there any other business members would like to bring up for discussion?"

Reidun clenched her fists as the silence stretched for an eternity. Time was running out. She had to say something. She couldn't do it. She'd make a complete fool of herself again.

She squeezed her eyes shut and forced her hand into the air.

Oskar said, "I see we have a question. Yes, there in the back of the room."

Opening her eyes, Reidun swallowed hard and prepared to speak.

But someone else was talking. Steinar? She whirled around to see him on his feet.

"Thanks for the chance to speak. Last month, you appointed me to lead a sub-committee to investigate whether it's feasible for Berghaven to have its own Christmas fair. The report was completed and presented to you. I and other members of this chamber would like an update about what follow-up action the executive committee plans to take in the light of the report."

Oskar crossed his arms. "We're looking into it."

"I appreciate that," Steinar said. "But it's already the tail end of September, and I thought we need to act quickly. Wasn't this Christmas fair an event we were considering holding this year?"

Steinar looked around as though to read the room, and Reidun saw several heads nodding.

Oskar must have seen it, too. "I'll make sure every member of the chamber of commerce gets a copy of the report. Thanks for your input. And now, I have to bring this meeting to—"

"And what about follow-up actions?" Steinar spoke again. "Time is running short."

Oskar's eyes flashed. "You want follow-up actions? Okay. See me immediately after this. Ladies and gentlemen, I'll now call this meeting to a close."

Reidun knew that look on Oskar's face. He was angry. But why? He was going to speak to Steinar after the meeting, but he hadn't asked her to join. She would wait and find out what they said.

Steinar crossed his arms, watching Oskar shuffle documents into his briefcase. The post-meeting buzz filled the air as members of Berghaven's business community moved around them.

Finally, Oskar straightened up and gave his friend a long stare. "I thought I made it clear when we last spoke that there are reasons I'm moving cautiously on this matter. I'm disappointed that you found it necessary to force the issue in front of everyone."

Steinar's face burned, but he kept his tone even. "I'm sorry you see it that way. But it's an urgent issue since there's not much time left before Christmas. There are people whose income depends on Christmas sales.

Reidun told me there are several vendors who are keen to participate. I thought we owed it to them to at least hear what's going on."

Oskar nodded slowly. "Ah, Reidun. Of course."

Steinar frowned. "Excuse me?"

Oskar chuckled. "Now I get it. But I don't blame you. She has a way about her."

"I don't understand what you mean." Steinar's face was on fire.

Oskar grinned. "This was her idea from the beginning, and you've been backing her from day one. Why else would you be so invested in this?"

"The only reason I'm invested is because it's a good idea, and I think it would be good for the community."

Steinar clenched his fists as Oskar continued to smirk at him.

"Fine," Oskar said. "Let's see how to make this happen. We have an events committee, but the chairperson has a lot on her plate right now. The timing isn't ideal."

He gestured toward a young woman who stood a few feet away.

Glancing at her, Steinar caught sight of her very round belly.

"Kjersti is due to have her baby within the next couple of weeks," Oskar said. "She'd normally take the lead on things like this, but I can't ask her to take on that responsibility right now. So, since you're so eager to see this happen, I'll nominate you to head a steering committee to organize the Christmas fair."

"Me?" Steinar echoed.

"Yes, you. You'll have to see about planning permission from the town council and carry out all the fundraising." He gave Steinar a wintry smile. "Because, of course you realize the chamber of commerce has no budget to cover this event. You'll need to send me progress updates every week so I can be sure everything is on track. I'll call an extraordinary meeting of the executive committee within the next couple of days to authorize all of this. Expect terms of reference within the week."

Steinar nodded. What had he gotten himself into? He'd only wanted to make sure that Reidun's idea got a proper hearing. He hadn't expected to actually have to put the fair together, including somehow finding the money to fund it. "Will the executive committee nominate other people to help me out, or shall I—"

Oskar snapped his briefcase shut. "You may choose your own helpers, as long as they're members in good standing of the chamber of commerce. Send me their names as soon as you can, so I can make the terms of reference include them. Are you happy now? Is this all moving fast enough for you?"

Steinar bristled at his friend's tone, but kept his expression bland. "It is. Thanks once again."

"Good. I'm sure Reidun will be thrilled to hear this." Oskar shot him another look and then walked away before Steinar could reply.

Steinar stood where he was, his mind reeling at the responsibility he'd just taken on himself.

"What did Oskar have to say?"

Reidun stood a few feet away.

Steinar sighed. "He's dropped the whole thing in my lap and asked me to organize the fair. Without a budget."

Reidun's eyes widened. Then she grinned and punched the air. "Yes! It's going to be the best thing ever. Havdal are going to be so sorry that they treated us like trash."

Despite his misgivings, her excitement made Steinar smile. Oskar was right. This woman had a way about her.

"Well, I'm glad you're pleased about this, because you're going to help me," he said.

"Of course I am. When do we start? There's so much to do."

"I know. I'm trying to get my head around it." He pushed a hand through his hair. "The first thing we need to do is get people to help us. Can you think of any names? Oh, and Oskar insists that they need to be members of the chamber of commerce."

She nodded eagerly. "Of course. We should definitely ask Axel Vikham-mer. You met him and his wife Sonia at church. He owns the Community Arts Center, and that might be a resource we could use. She is a profes-sional fund-raiser and one of my best friends. And there are a few other people we could ask. Or beg."

He smiled. "Good. Would you please go ahead with that immedi-ately? Let me know as soon as you get confirmation, and then we can plan our first meeting."

"On it." She started to walk away, then turned to look at him over her shoulder. "I'm really excited about this. It's going to be amazing!"

He watched her go. He really hoped so.

Chapter Ten

WHY HAD HE LET himself get roped into this? Steinar followed the directions of the receptionist at the Berghaven Community Arts Center and headed toward the conference room.

Passing an open door, he glimpsed a pottery class. From the end of the hallway, a choir sang vocal warm-up exercises.

Organizing this Christmas fair was a fool's errand. Oskar was expecting this to fail—he'd all but admitted it. By giving the committee no budget and no other resources, he'd thrown Steinar in at the deep end. And if the fair failed to come off, Oskar could easily say it wasn't his fault.

Steinar was a stranger in this town, and all he had to work with was the team Reidun had pulled together. He needed all the help heaven could give.

Steinar pushed open the door of the conference room.

Four people were already sitting at the table. His gaze went straight to Reidun, who gave him an ear-to-ear grin and a wave.

She sat next to a woman who he thought he'd seen in church. Actually, looking around the table, he knew all of them from church, although he didn't remember everyone's names.

"Sorry, am I late?" he asked.

Reidun chuckled. "You're on time. We were all early. Since I asked everyone personally to join our group and we all know each other, maybe I should introduce them to you?"

"That sounds good," Steinar said. "I know all your faces from church and probably even said hello, but introductions would really help."

"Cool. First, Axel Vikhammer. He's a software developer and owns this community center."

Axel, a bespectacled, dark-haired man, nodded his head.

Reidun gestured toward a striking, dark-skinned woman sitting next to

Axel. "That's Sonia Krogstad-Vikhammer, Axel's wife. She's a public relations specialist and has a ton of experience in fund-raising. She's the reason the community arts center still exists. Since we're on our own financially, I'm really glad she's agreed to join us. We'll need all the help we can muster."

Steinar returned Sonia's smile. Fund-raising was not his forte, so it was a relief to hear there was someone who knew what she was doing.

His gaze went to the woman who sat beside Reidun.

Reidun inclined her head. "This is Bethany Meland. She works with the Berghaven Post and will be a big help to get the word out."

Bethany leaned forward. "There are still many people who read the paper, and there's always a positive response to community events."

Steinar looked around the table. "It's wonderful to meet all of you, and I'm very grateful that you joined us at such short notice. I imagine you're all very busy."

Sonia shrugged. "When Reidun told us what was going on and what she was doing about it, we all wanted to help. Berghaven should have had a Christmas fair ages ago, and I don't know why nobody ever thought of it."

"It's because Havdal is getting a bit too big for its britches," Reidun said. "When they were nice to us, we never thought of starting our own thing.

Why don't you introduce yourself to everyone, Steinar?"

"Of course. I'm Steinar Jakobsen and I'm an independent digital advertising specialist." He hesitated. There was no need to tell them what he used to do in England. It wasn't relevant for this task, anyway. "I have roots in West Finnmark, but I lived in England for many years. After my wife passed, I moved my family back here."

He cleared his throat. "I'll be honest with you. I have little experience doing anything like this, so I'm excited that you all have some area of expertise that will come in extremely useful. So, where do we start? You must be as insane as I am, because you've agreed to help plan and organize a

Christmas fair in under three months."

Sonia raised her hand. "If I may. I've done similar projects before and roughed out a plan of action. It sounds to me like we need to frame this as a community-building event, although of course we want the local business community to benefit. The first thing we need to do is work out a budget. We'll need funds to pay for permits, decorations, entertainment, and security, just to name a few. How will we raise that money? There are options, of course, but we'll need to decide quickly."

Steinar sat back, impressed by Sonia's confident tone.

She went on. "We have to pick a date and a venue ASAP. Will it be indoors or outdoors? How many people are we expecting? Will it be a one-day or multi-day event? These are all decisions we have to make very soon."

She glanced at her notebook and flipped over a page. "Then there are the permits. We'll need permits if we want to use public spaces, and permits to serve food and beverages. And we also have to decide what activities and entertainment we're going to have, and schedule those. As an aside, the community arts center has an incredible youth choir who I think would love to be involved. Right, Axel?"

Axel smiled at his wife. "I think they would."

She returned Axel's smile, then looked at Steinar. "And then, of course, we'll have to get vendors involved. I think Reidun will be on top of this, since she knows a lot of the vendors who regularly participate in Havdal's Christmas fair."

"I'm happy to take responsibility for that," Reidun said. "And to work out where any gaps might be so we don't have ten booths selling mittens."

"Brilliant. We'll need lots of volunteers to help as well with things like cleanup, setting up the area, and decorating. Plus a marketing plan, of course. And this goes back to the funding issue. Are we going to approach local businesses to sponsor us? They could either support us with money or in kind, or with their services."

Bethany broke in. "Like ask a florist to support us by decorating for free? I could see if the newspaper might give us a bit of ad space in addition to stories we'll run."

"Yes, exactly that," Sonia said. "That's just the tip of the iceberg. I've not even talked about how we'll handle communication among all the people we hope to involve, and the coordination all of this will take. My husband might be able to help with all the techy stuff that involves."

Steinar removed his glasses and stared at Sonia. "If you want to take over the chair in this committee, I'll gladly step aside. You're on top of everything we need to do."

She laughed. "I have no interest in taking the lead on the actual work. I was just mapping out the way forward."

"Even though it's clearly going to be a ton of work, I feel a lot more confident." Steinar turned to Reidun. "You've assembled a crack team. Well done."

Reidun beamed.

Steinar looked around the room. "All right, then. I'll feel a lot better if we can make some of those big decisions Sonia talked about before we leave today. Let's get straight into planning."

Chapter Eleven

"REIDUN, ARE YOU OKAY?" Steinar glanced at her as they walked down the glossy marble corridor of Berghaven's Town Hall. Two weeks after their first steering committee meeting, they were here to try and win the town council's support for Berghaven's first ever Christmas fair.

"I'm okay," Reidun said, her voice tight. "Why?" She kept up a brisk pace, her long stride matching his.

He shrugged. "I don't know. Maybe because you dropped your keys twice on the way up the stairs. And the receptionist had to chase after you with the purse you left on her desk when we were signing into the building."

As she turned to face him her keys slid to the floor with a loud clatter that echoed against the walls.

He picked them up and held them out to her. "Three times."

Her fingers were trembling as she took the keys away and stuffed them into her bag, her face averted.

She started to walk off again, but he touched her arm. "Reidun, I can tell something's wrong. What is it?"

Still looking away, she crossed her arms tightly across her body. "Give me a moment, okay?"

"Okay." He held his hands up and stepped away. They didn't really have a moment, though. Not when the council was expecting them to give their pitch in ten minutes.

He was about to speak to her again when she mumbled something, her back still toward him.

He moved closer. "What did you say?"

Her shoulders sagged. "I said someone else should give the presentation to the town council."

"What?" He stared at her back. "We agreed you were the best choice." Was she really getting cold feet when they were about to go into their meeting?

She turned around slowly, raising her gaze to meet his.

His objections froze on his lips. Was she... scared?

She drew in a shaky breath. "I know I agreed to do this. But I'm terrible at giving speeches. You saw me speaking at the chamber of commerce. It was a complete shambles, and the only reason they listened was because you made my points in a more articulate way. We can't afford to mess up this chance with the town council. We should have arranged for you to do it. Or Sonia. She's a natural at speaking in public."

She turned away, her body rigid.

"Reidun, listen," he said. "You're the perfect member of the team to convince the town council to support our Christmas fair. You'll bring an authenticity that neither I nor Sonia can match. Sonia may have experience in public speaking and I may be the chair, but you're part of the business community this fair is going to help. You're one of the vendors who's had to go all the way to Havdal to have access to the Christmas trade."

She shook her head as though she wasn't convinced.

He touched her shoulder, and she looked at him, her brown eyes troubled. "I really wish I hadn't volunteered."

The uncertainty in her face stirred something deep inside him. She could hold up traffic in order to tow a stranded car without blinking an eye, but saying a few words to a group of town councilors had her doubting herself. What a strange mix of toughness and vulnerability. He squeezed her shoulder. "I know you can do it. You believe in what we're doing, and I believe in you. Just relax and be yourself. Speak slowly. And pretend the council members all have rubber chickens on their heads."

A tiny smile curved her lips.

"I'll pray for you quickly now, okay?" He squeezed her shoulder again, and she nodded and bowed her head.

"Dear Father," he prayed, "you know Reidun is really struggling. We ask that you would calm her nerves, fill her with peace, and let her words flow. Help her speak from her heart and bring her points out with clarity and eloquence. Thank you for this opportunity to share our vision with the town council. Help us both to do our best, and to leave the results in your hands. We ask in Jesus' name. Amen."

"Amen." She looked up at him, blinking quickly, her eyes moist. "That was a beautiful prayer. Thank you."

"You're welcome. Are you ready to go in?"

Drawing a deep breath, she balled her hands into fists. "Okay. Let's go."

"That's the spirit. You've got this."

They walked into the conference room where the councilors waited for them.

Steinar prayed under his breath as the mayor welcomed them and invited them to address the meeting.

He got to his feet. "Thanks so much for taking the time to listen to us. My name is Steinar Jakobsen and this is my colleague Reidun Norberg. We're here on behalf of Berghaven's chamber of commerce with an exciting proposal that we hope will win your interest and support. I'll step aside and let Reidun have the floor."

She shot him a quick glance, and he poured all his encouragement into a smile.

Her hands trembled as she straightened her jacket, but her voice was steady as she started to speak.

His gaze was fixed on her face as she asked Berghaven's town council to lend its support to the town's first Christmas fair.

She hit every point their team had discussed, and by the time she wound down her speech, several councilors nodded along.

"In conclusion, this Christmas fair will build community in Berghaven, give exposure to local businesses, and boost tourism. We hope that the town council will throw its weight behind this event, giving us the necessary permits and smoothing any logistical hurdles. Thank you for your attention."

Applause rang around the room as she sank into her chair.

Steinar did a mental fist pump. She'd totally nailed it.

The mayor stood and inclined his head toward them. "Thanks for your presentation, Reidun. Ladies and gentlemen, are there any questions or points on which you want more clarification?"

As a councilor got to his feet to speak, Reidun pressed a note into Steinar's hand.

He glanced at it. It was a doodle of a stick man with a chicken on his head.

Covering his mouth to hide a grin, he looked over at Reidun.

She gave him a quick wink.

Chapter Twelve

"**H**EY, LOOK, IT'S REIDUN! Isn't that Reidun?"

She halted mid-stride in the central concourse of the Berghaven mall and spun around at the sound of a high, piping voice yelling her name.

Steinar and his children stood outside the toy store. She hadn't seen him since the town council meeting a couple of days earlier.

Mya waved, a grin on her face. "I told you it was Reidun. Hi."

Reidun walked up to them. "Hi. How are you guys?"

Steinar said, "We're fine. Actually, we need a favor if you're not in a hurry. A couple of twins who shall remain nameless had massive mango smoothies and now both need the bathroom at the same time. Would you mind taking Mya to the ladies' bathroom?"

"Of course not."

"Thanks so much." He flashed her a smile. "You're a lifesaver. Shall we meet back out here?"

"Sure. Come on, Mya." Reidun held out her hand, then belatedly wondered whether that was the wrong thing to do. Were seven-year-olds too mature to hold a grown-up's hand?

Mya slipped her fingers into Reidun's hand and the two headed toward the escalator.

"So, um, have you been shopping?" Reidun asked.

"Yes."

"What did you get?"

"I got a birthday present for Randi. She's in my Sunday school class and also in my class at school. She invited me to her party next weekend."

"That sounds like fun. It's lovely to be invited to a party."

Mya smiled. "Yeah. Chase wasn't invited because he's a boy, but he's going to have a play date with Mattis, so that made him feel better. And last week he went to a party that I didn't get asked to."

"I'm glad to hear you're making friends."

They walked into the bathroom and Reidun pointed toward an empty stall. "Go in and I'll wait for you."

When Mya had finished, she came out and washed her hands at the sink. She threw Reidun a sidelong glance. "Thanks. I hate going to the men's bathrooms. They always stink."

Reidun laughed. "I know, right? When I was little, I sometimes had to go to the men's bathroom with my dad. He didn't have much of a choice since he couldn't bring me into the ladies' bathroom."

Mya stared at her. "Where was your mum?"

Reidun hesitated. There was no way she could explain to this little girl how her mother had dumped her at her father's doorstep and left without a backward glance. Best to keep things simple. "I didn't have one. So when we went out, my father had to figure out what to do about the bathroom."

"That's just like my dad." Mya shook the water off her hands. "Sometimes he stands outside and asks a random lady to take me inside. But if I really need to go and Chase also has to go, then he just takes us both into the men's bathroom. Or sometimes there's a big bathroom that's for people with disabilities, but Dad says we shouldn't use that in case someone else really needs it."

They went outside and headed toward the down escalator.

Chase and Steinar stood waiting outside the toy store.

Chase gave a theatrical sigh. "Finally! We've been waiting forever."

"It wasn't that long," Mya said.

Steinar smiled at Reidun. "Thanks so much. I really appreciate your help."

"Not a problem." She stood awkwardly for a moment, then gestured over her shoulder. "I'd better get going."

"Oh. We were on our way out, too," he said.

She fell into step with him as they headed toward the door. Since they were going the same way, it would be awkward to rush ahead or lag behind.

The cool breeze hit her face as she stepped out into the town square. Autumn was giving way to winter, and it was already getting darker.

"Dad, Dad, look. Can we go on that?" Chase pulled his father's hand.

Reidun followed where the little boy was pointing. Someone had set up a teacup ride in the square. A handful of children sat on the garishly colored ride, lights flashing while carnival music blared.

Mya backed up her brother's plea. "Please, Dad?"

"Sure, okay. Don't run too far ahead," he called out as the children raced toward the ride.

They slowed their pace to a fast walk.

Steinar looked at Reidun. "Are you thinking what I'm thinking?"

"That it would be a delightful addition to have rides like this at our Christmas fair?"

He grinned back. "Exactly. Let's find out who's in charge."

They walked up to the ride, where the twins stood at the back of a line of children who were waiting for the current cycle to stop. A young man with brown spiky hair collected payment from the customers.

When they reached the front of the line, Steinar pulled out his wallet. "Two children, please. Also, who can

I speak to about hiring a ride like this for an event I'm organizing?"

The young man took the payment and pointed over his shoulder. "You can ask the guy over there who's running the controls. Next, please."

Steinar, Reidun, and the children stepped out of the way.

Reidun turned to Steinar. "Shall I watch them while you talk to the guy in charge?"

"Would you? Thanks so much. Or you could talk to him and let me know what he says."

She shook her head. "No, you go ahead and find out."

Chase stood next to her, bouncing on the balls of his feet. She remembered what it was like to feel so excited about riding a spinning teacup.

The ride slowed to a stop, and the passengers climbed off.

The line of waiting children surged forward.

"I want a pink one," Mya said, clambering onto the ride.

Chase chose a green teacup.

Reidun looked over at Steinar. He was deep in conversation with the man at the control desk. The man gave him a card, which Steinar slipped into his pocket.

Steinar came back to Reidun as the ride cranked into motion.

"What did he say?"

"He said he works for a big company that hires out fairground rides for private and public events. I'll need to call their office on Monday, but it sounds like they're a solid outfit. Apparently, they do events like this all the time, but he said we need to be quick if we want something around Christmas before they all get booked up. We might already be late."

"Does 'late' mean we get the boring rides?" Reidun asked.

"Or no rides at all. I'll be on it first thing on Monday."

They both turned to look at the children and Steinar whipped his phone out, snapping pictures of them as they whirled around on the ride.

She glanced at him. "I don't know how you do it."

"Do what?"

"Parent your children, run a small business. Have a life."

His mouth tipped upward. "Who said I have a life?"

She smiled back. "Well, you know what I mean. It must be pretty full on. I'm impressed by how you balance it all."

He looked away, stuffing his hands in his pockets. Had she said something wrong?

The thudding beat of the pop tune filled the air, but it was Steinar's extended silence that filled her ears. She'd definitely put her foot in it. She'd better excuse herself now, because there was no reason to linger on. "Well, I have to—"

"Sorry, it's just—"

Steinar's words came at the same time as hers.

He flushed and said, "I'm sorry. Go ahead."

"No, you go ahead."

"Okay." He cleared his throat. "Thanks for your compliment. It's hard to know how to take it because I'm never sure whether I've got the balance right. Charlotte was the hands-on parent while I worked all day. She kept the children fed and clean, took care of all the home stuff and the discipline. All I had to do was the fun things in the evenings. Bed-time stories, a quick prayer before they went to sleep. She was carrying the load, and I only learned how much she did when she got sick. It was a rude awakening to do everything alone, and realize that I'm not actually dad of the year. It's easy to be fun dad. Not so easy to actually parent when your children are fighting over the most idiotic things, you're afraid you're scarring them for life, and you can't even go to the bathroom in peace."

Reidun swallowed. How did she respond to that?

He flushed a deeper shade of red. "Oops. Did all that come out aloud?"

"Tough parenting day?"

He chuckled. "Does it show?"

"Well, I still think you're doing a fantastic job. I don't have experience, obviously, but anyone can see that the children are thriving."

"Thanks," he said.

They watched the children for a moment and she sneaked a glance at his profile, her gaze tracing his firm jaw and the contours of his mouth. His mouth? Really?

He turned toward her and her face grew hot. Thank goodness mind reading wasn't a thing.

"Speaking of jobs," he said, "I wanted to ask you something."

"Sure. Go ahead."

"I seem to have an issue with one of my toilets. I noticed this morning that the cistern keeps running. Is that something your company deals with, or do you only work with big corporate clients?"

He was asking her to fix his toilet? That was the perfect antidote to stop her mind from drifting where it shouldn't. Focus on the man's leaking water closets instead of picturing what it would be like to—

"A leaking toilet, you said?" And now she was talking far too loud. "We don't normally work on the weekend, but I don't mind having a quick look at it now just to be sure it's not a major issue."

His eyes widened. "Would you? I don't mean to put you out. And of course I'll pay your regular call-out rate."

"It's not a problem. Text me your address and I'll nip home and grab my equipment."

"I really appreciate that. I'll message you right now."

"Okay, then. See you in about half an hour?"

"See you then."

Chapter Thirteen

ER TOOLBOX IN HAND, Reidun wiped her feet on the brown herringbone doormat and rang Steinar's doorbell.

She looked around her as she waited for him to answer. After years of visits to people's homes, she had a long-standing theory that you could often tell a lot about a person by their front yard.

What did Steinar Jakobsen's front yard say about him? It was neat and uncluttered, with just a few autumn leaves lying across an otherwise well-swept driveway. Two children's bicycles leaned against the wall, and three pairs of muddy wellington boots lined up next to the door. Two small ones in purple and green, and one pair of extra large gray ones.

So, he liked to spend time outdoors with his children, and he had modest and subdued tastes. Perhaps he didn't have time to fuss around with extravagant decor, but he valued neatness enough to keep it presentable.

The door opened, and she looked down into Chase's wide blue eyes.

"Hi, Reidun. Are you going to fix our toilet?"

"Chase, you're not supposed to open the—oh, hi, Reidun." Steinar came down the hallway and stood behind his son.

Chase turned around. "But I knew she was coming."

"It doesn't matter. Only big kids and adults answer the doorbell, okay? Please come in."

Steinar stepped aside and made room for her to enter.

How did a single guy with two children have such an elegant and tidy home? A delicious aroma of something meaty and spicy filled the air. He could cook, too?

He was too good to be true. She needed to focus on what had brought her here.

"Where's the patient?" she asked.

He stared at her for a moment, his face blank. Then he slapped his forehead with his palm and chuckled. "You mean the leaky toilet, right?"

"Sorry. Plumber humor. Yes, I mean the toilet."

Chase answered, his words tumbling out. "It's the one upstairs. It keeps on running and Dad says it's going to waste water. Can I watch?"

She smiled. "Yes, of course, if your dad doesn't mind. Can you take me to where it is?"

"And make sure you keep out of the way," Steinar said.

Reidun followed the boy up the stairs and into a large family bathroom decorated in gray and light blue.

It had a bathtub, shower cabinet, and the offending toilet.

Leaning against the bathtub, Chase pointed to the toilet tank. "Can you hear that?"

Reidun tilted her head. The sound of running water was loud and clear. "I can indeed."

She put her toolbox down. "The first thing I need to do is shut off the water."

Crouching down, she scanned the area on the floor behind the toilet. Whoa. Steinar's bathroom was incredibly clean. She'd seen a lot of nasty bathrooms in the course of her work, but this one was impressive. Either he employed an excellent cleaner or he was meticulous. She found the valve to cut off the flow of water.

Straightening up, she spoke to Chase even though she sensed Steinar's presence behind her. "Let's have a look inside the tank now. It could be a few things. They're all relatively easy fixes, but I might need to go back for the parts I need."

As she lifted the ceramic lid off the cistern, she glimpsed Steinar filling the doorway, his gaze on her.

Chase leaned closer as she put the lid on the floor. "We'll need to be very careful with this lid, because it can break. We'll make sure to put it out of the way."

"Okay," Chase said. "Do you know what's wrong yet?"

She turned back to the toilet. "When I'm trying to figure out what the problem is, I like to start with the simplest options first. There's something in here called a fill valve, which helps control how the water fills this tank. This is the water that whooshes through when you flush the toilet. And after you flush, it has to fill up again."

She lifted the float above the water. Chase's warm breath stirred her arm.

"Oh, I see what's wrong. Luckily, it's simple. I think I just need to adjust the float. I'll just use a screwdriver to lower the float cap below the overflow tube." She grabbed her screwdriver and made a quick adjustment to the spline. "And...we're done."

"That's it?" Steinar's voice rumbled from behind her.

"Yes, that's it. I'll just replace the tank cover, and that will be all."

"Wow. I was expecting you might need to take the whole thing apart."

She smiled. "Thankfully, not this time. I'll turn the water back on again and we can test everything."

When the water was on, she pointed to the tank. "See, Chase? No more leaking through."

She replaced the lid on the tank and put her screwdriver back into her toolbox. "I'm glad it wasn't more serious."

Steinar said, "How much do I owe you for the call-out?"

"You can't be serious. That took all of five minutes to sort out, including walking up your stairs."

He shook his head. "Still, it was a disruption of your day, and you fixed the problem. Please. I insist."

She sighed. "Okay, have it your way. I'll email you an invoice first thing in the morning."

"Thanks. And one more thing." He hesitated as he looked at her. "I was about to serve dinner. Would you like to stay and eat with us?"

She grasped for her toolbox as it slipped from her hand. "Oh. Thank you. That's very kind of you."

"Good." A smile spread over his face.

"I'll just wash my hands."

"The living room is over to the right when you come down the stairs. I'll set an extra place."

He left, and she turned to the sink.

A thrill of excitement shot through her. It would be wonderful to spend the evening with Steinar and his children. But she needed to be sensible. She couldn't read too much into this. The worst thing she could do was misinterpret his intentions and make a fool of herself.

She needed to treat it as a meal with her colleague and his children.

She shut off the water and dried her hands on a guest towel that hung next to the sink. Wow, that was really soft. How did he get his towels so fluffy?

As she walked down the stairs, a portrait on the wall snagged her gaze. A woman of exquisite beauty sat with two small children. Her luscious waves of blond hair reminded Reidun of a picture of a fairy princess she'd once seen in a storybook. The pale, filmy fabric of her dress added to the ethereal quality of her face. Every feature was perfection, from her wide, blue eyes to her smile. This must be Steinar's wife.

The children were, of course, Mya and Chase, aged about two. Mya sat on her mother's knee and Chase stood next to his mother, his pudgy hand on her shoulder. They looked so much like her. Steinar must see her every time he looked into their faces.

Reidun stared at the picture. What had she been like? She looked young. Much younger than Steinar. She must have been a good mother to have raised such sweet children. And to have captured Steinar's heart.

Steinar's voice jolted her. "Wash up for dinner, children."

She tore her gaze away from the picture.

The living room wasn't hard to find. It was a large, open plan space. An L-shaped sofa and a couple of armchairs were grouped around a coffee table. The dining table stood on the other side of the room.

Mya slid into a chair, and Chase sat opposite her.

Reidun set her toolbox down and took a couple of steps closer.

Steinar emerged from a doorway on the right, holding a large pot with oven mitts. He smiled at Reidun. "Grab a seat."

He put the pot on the table and slid the oven mitts off. "I'll grab the bread."

Reidun settled into her seat.

Steinar came out of the kitchen with a basket of rolls, which he set on the table. "Here we go. Let's give thanks."

Reidun bowed her head along with everyone else.

Steinar was silent for an instant, then prayed, "Thank you, Lord, for this lovely day. Thanks for this meal and for our guest who is here to share it with us. We are grateful for all your gifts. In Jesus' name. Amen."

"Amen," Chase echoed, grabbing for a roll.

Mya shot him a glare. "Chase, you're supposed to offer things to your guests first."

The little boy colored, but Reidun could relate. She knew how easy it was to forget her own manners when food was involved. "He's probably as hungry as I am," she said.

Chase held the basket out to her. "Would you care for a roll, miss?"

She suppressed a smile at his over the top politeness. Someone had trained him very well. "Yes, please. Thank you very much."

Steinar held out his hand. "Pass me your bowls and I'll give you some stew."

Reidun sniffed at her full bowl when Mya passed it back to her. "This smells incredible. What do you call it?"

"I don't think it has a special name. It's just beef stew with potatoes, carrots, and a few herbs."

She took a bite, closing her eyes to savor the glorious melding of flavors. "You actually made this?"

He smiled. "It's one of the talents I discovered in the past couple of years. I never suspected I would enjoy cooking. Do you cook?"

She wished she could say yes, but she had to be honest. "Making a sandwich is about the limit of my abilities. My friend Johanna is a brilliant cook, and she's tried to teach me many times, but it's never clicked."

"You're very good at fixing a toilet, though." Chase looked at her from behind his half-eaten roll.

Reidun grinned. "Yes, I can do that."

"And you can run a tow truck," Mya added.

"I can do that, too."

The little girl looked at Reidun with solemn eyes. "Everyone has something they can do. God made us all good at something. So, it's okay if you're not good at everything."

Reidun held back a chuckle as the seven-year-old dispensed wisdom. It was true, after all, even though the speaker still had a mouthful of baby teeth. "You're absolutely right, Mya. What are you good at?"

Mya slid a spoonful of stew into her mouth and chewed slowly, her gaze directed upward. She looked back at Reidun. "I'm good at reading. And drawing."

"How about you, Chase?"

"I'm good with Legos and at running and soccer."

"Those are great abilities to have," Reidun said. She dipped the roll in her bowl and ate another delicious mouthful.

"You didn't ask me what else I'm good at."

Reidun looked at Steinar and he stared back at her, his mouth tilted upward.

"Sorry, I didn't," she said. "What else are you good at?"

"I can do magic tricks. Or, rather, sleight of hand."

Mya's eyes lit up. "Oh, yeah, Dad can make it look like something disappeared. I don't know how he does it."

Reidun faced Steinar again. "Really? I'm pretty good at those kinds of tricks myself."

He grinned. "Challenge accepted. Let's have a magic trick duel after dinner, and the children can judge between us."

Reidun gave him her best game face. "It's on."

"Yay!" Mya clapped her hands.

Reidun finished her stew and happily accepted a second bowlful. She would have asked Steinar for the recipe if she was any good at making food. But when she tried to follow recipes, something always went awry.

She sighed and pushed her bowl away. "That was really good."

Chase dabbed at his mouth with a napkin. "No dessert today, so you don't need to save up room. We only get dessert once a week."

"Is that so?" Reidun twirled her spoon. That was one way to cut down on naughty treats.

"Yes. Dad says we only get dessert on Sunday. But if you come for dinner then, you could get dessert."

Reidun's face heated. She hoped Steinar wouldn't imagine she was angling for an invite.

He didn't appear to have heard, though. He gathered the bowls and spoons and ferried them to the kitchen.

"Magic duel!" Mya said. "Shall we do it in the living room?"

Steinar walked past his daughter and stroked her hair. "Yes, that'll be good. We'll start as soon as I clear the table."

He faced Reidun, pointing a finger toward her nose. "And you'd better prepare your best tricks because you are going down."

Reidun and the children were seated on the sofa when Steinar strode into the living room with a flourish.

"Ladies and gentleman, prepare to be amazed. The Incredible Fantastico is going to stun and delight you with his stupendous and wonderful skill."

Reidun cupped her hands around her mouth. "Boo! Less talking, more showing."

Steinar drew himself up to his full height, giving his best impression of offended dignity. "Do you doubt my abilities? Prepare to be dazzled, I say."

He held up a coin. "I shall now make this coin... disappear!"

With dramatic hand waving and waggling of his fingers, he made a show of moving the coin from one hand to another in a classic false transfer, then held up the hand where the audience expected the coin to be. It was now clearly empty.

Chase and Mya clapped.

He turned toward Reidun. "Are you prepared to acknowledge the awe-inspiring skill of the Incredible Fantastico?"

She feigned a yawn. "Not bad for a basic trick. But now I'll show you how the pros do it. Do you have a pack of playing cards?"

"I'll get it." Chase jumped to his feet and raced to the bookshelf. He came back with a pack of plastic-covered cards that he handed to Reidun.

"Thanks. Now, I'll need a volunteer."

"Me!" Chase and Mya shouted at the same time.

Reidun stroked her chin. "Hm, how should we decide? Rock paper scissors?"

Mya nodded. "Okay."

She and her brother did the classic dueling hand game, which Chase won after a couple of tries.

"Aw, man!" Scowling, Mya sank into her chair, her arms crossed.

Uh oh. Steinar hoped Mya wouldn't sink into a sulk.

Reidun leaned toward the girl. "Don't worry. I can do the trick twice if you like, and you can volunteer the second time. Chase will go first."

Mya's face brightened. "Okay."

The cards in her hand, Reidun faced the children. "Madame Reidun the Renowned shall now dazzle you with her power. But first, the Inedible Fantastico must make way for my greatness."

Steinar crossed his arms. "It's the Incredible Fantastico."

"That's what I said. The Indelible Fantastico." She grinned. "Excuse me, please. Such awesomeness as mine needs space to operate. Please take your seat."

The children giggled as Steinar joined them on the sofa.

Reidun turned to face Chase. "Pick a card. Any card." She held the deck out to him.

Chase slipped a card out.

"Good. Now, look at it and memorize what it is. Don't show me."

The boy stared at his card.

"I, Madame Reidun, am now going to flip over every card in the deck except for the one Chase chose. Are you ready?"

"Boo! No." Steinar grinned at her. How did she like being heckled?

She shot him a glare. "I will astound the doubters. Slip your card back in the deck, Chase. Thank you. Now, clap your hands once."

As Chase clapped, she slammed the cards down on the table. When she spread them out, all of them were face up, apart from one. She picked the one that was face down. "Is this your card?"

Chase stared at her, mouth agape. "Yes! How did you do that?"

"Madame Reidun the Renowned does not reveal her secrets."

"My turn to pick a card," Mya said.

"Okay. I'll shuffle the deck first. Here you go."

Steinar watched as she did the trick again. Once more, his children stared in amazement.

She smirked at Steinar. "Do you concede my victory?"

"No, never," he said. "Can you do this?" It was from the bottom of the barrel, but he did the good old thumb removal trick, which his children cheered as though it wasn't the fiftieth time they were seeing it.

Reidun waved away the applause. "If you think that was good, how about this?" She grabbed a pen off the table. Facing the children and Steinar, she made it appear as though the pen disappeared from her hand. Then she created the illusion of pulling it out of her nose.

"Ew!" Chase shouted. "That's gross!"

"Do I win, though?"

Steinar laughed. "You win. I can't top that."

"Good." She chuckled. "Because I don't know any other tricks."

Steinar's sides ached. It felt so good to laugh with someone.

"You've got to show me how you do that card trick," he said.

"Okay, here's how you do it."

As the children looked on eagerly, Reidun demonstrated how she flipped the cards over cleverly so that, no matter which card the volunteer picked, it would always show up facing the opposite way to the other cards. The trick was simple once you knew how to do it, but clever and impressive.

It had been a long time since Steinar had enjoyed an evening like this with anyone. And his children were having fun, too.

He watched Reidun as she taught his children the trick, going through each step slowly and carefully. Their blond heads leaned closer, contrasting against her black hair, their pale faces and hands setting off her mahogany-colored skin. They didn't look like a family. But, for an instant, they felt like one.

Something clicked, as though a blurry image had fallen into focus. Reidun... a family. Could it—

"Yay, I did it!" Mya yelled as she slapped the deck of cards on the table. She beamed at Reidun.

"You got the hang of it faster than I did," Reidun said. "I won't tell you how many tries it took me."

Chase looked up at Reidun. "Can you teach us how to do the pen up the nose trick?"

She smiled back at him as she gathered up the cards. "Yes, but I'm afraid it'll have to be another time. It's getting late."

"Promise?" Chase asked.

Steinar walked forward. "We'll sort out when that will happen. Children, you'd better get ready for bed. Clean your teeth and I'll be up soon.

Reidun stood. "Thanks for dinner. Bye, children."

"Thanks for fixing the toilet," Chase said as he headed toward the stairs.

Mya waved. "And thanks for teaching us that trick. I'm going to show Randi at school."

"I'll walk you to the door," Steinar said.

She picked up her toolbox, and he followed her to the front door and out onto the doorstep.

Pulling the door closed behind him, he said, "I had a wonderful time tonight."

She smiled, looking at him. "Me too."

"I'd like to learn the pen up the nose trick, too. Before you teach the children. Maybe you could show me over dinner sometime?"

He held his breath as he waited for her reaction.

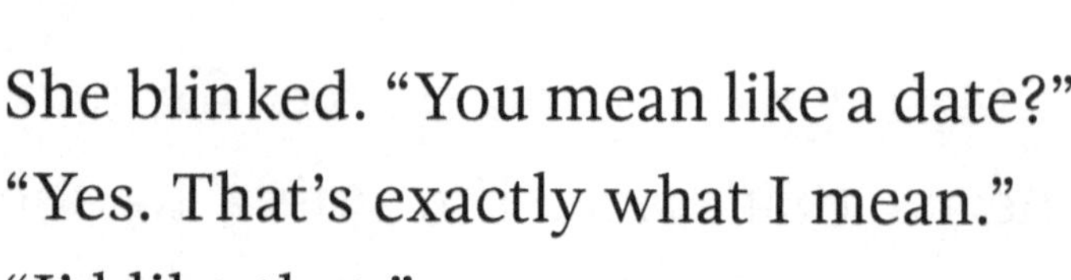

She blinked. "You mean like a date?"

"Yes. That's exactly what I mean."

"I'd like that."

His heart sang as the tension left his body. "That's great. Is Saturday night good? I can pick you up at your place."

"Sounds good. See you Saturday. Good night."

Chapter Fourteen

EIDUN'S HEART RACED as she walked back to her truck. She felt like she was floating three feet above the driveway.

During this evening with Steinar and his children, she'd glimpsed a tantalizing hope. A brief vision of herself as part of a family, not just on the outside looking in. And now, Steinar had asked her on a date.

She opened the back passenger door of her truck and put her toolbox inside.

Steinar was funny, charming, and smart. She'd loved spending time with him and his children. But he'd lost his wife not too long ago. His beautiful wife who had stayed at home to look after him and their children. Was he really over her? And his children had lost their mother.

This wasn't as simple as going on a date. The stakes were too high.

She fired up her engine and started the drive back home. A single father with small children. Could she really afford to let her heart get tangled up in that? To have something she yearned for dangled before her eyes only to lose it all?

As her headlights illuminated the road ahead, she recognized the blind corner where she'd run into Steinar and his children for the first time.

She slowed her truck down, and her gaze swept over the spot where his car had been stranded.

Lord, is this your doing?

She didn't get a reply to her silent prayer.

The muted pastel and gray color palette and candlelit ambiance of La Belle Saison were supposed to exude romance and sophistication, but the restaurant's charm was doing nothing for Reidun.

She stole a glance at Steinar over the menu and caught him sneaking a look at her. Her face burst into flame as she whipped her gaze away.

She needed to get a grip. She was a mature, full-grown woman, not a fourteen-year-old. She should have left all that awkwardness behind her decades ago. Steinar wasn't a stranger, and they'd been working together for some time. Their last evening with the children had been fun and relaxing.

But now the word "date" loomed over them, with all its implications. Since Steinar had picked her up from her doorstep tonight, she'd felt like an ungainly, coltish girl who didn't know what to do with her hands and who couldn't think of anything intelligent to say. What if tonight led nowhere? Or... what if it led somewhere?

The conversation never got off the ground, but limped along, lurching from comments about the weather to speculating on Tromsø Idrettslag's chances of pulling off an upset in tonight's Elite Series soccer game.

When she heard herself inquiring about the health of his toilet, Reidun knew something had to give. She could either cringe her way through the rest of the evening or face her awkwardness head on.

She cleared her throat. "I've got a confession to make."

"Oh? What?" He adjusted a spoon on the tablecloth.

"This is the first date I've been on in over twenty years. And I'm not sure how to carry myself."

He smiled. "It's been about eighteen years for me. I'm pretty rusty as well. I guess it shows."

"So, we can both agree that this date isn't going particularly well."

He folded his hands. "Maybe the best thing to do is to own the weirdness and just be honest. Talk to each other like grown-ups."

"Own the weirdness. I like that," she said. "I've never been good at being coy or subtle, and I'm too old to begin now. So, can we start the evening over? Let's pretend the previous half hour never happened, and I didn't ask you about your plumbing."

He threw his head back and laughed, and the tight knot in her gut eased up.

"Let's start from square one," she said. "We're here because we want to get to know a bit more about each other."

"Okay, let's do that." Steinar leveled his gaze at her, his face getting serious. "And we might as well start with the big things. Do you want to know anything about Charlotte and me?"

The menu slid from her fingers. The man got straight to the point with this being honest thing. "You and Charlotte? I admit, I have wondered a few things."

"You're free to ask."

"Thanks." She fidgeted with the fancy tassel on her menu. What should she ask about? There was a world of things she was dying to know about his late wife. "Um... well, I saw her picture on the wall in your house. She looked very young. Was there a big age difference?"

Steinar nodded. "Fourteen years. I was thirty-five, and she was twenty-one when we were married. We met about a year before that."

Reidun swallowed. "That means she must have only been in her thirties when she—um..." she trailed off.

"When she died? Yes. She was thirty-six."

"That was brutally young."

He sighed. "It was. Thirty-six years feels like nothing. I learned to see Psalm 90:12 in a whole new way. 'Teach us to number our days, that we may apply our hearts to wisdom.'"

Reidun's fingers tightened around her menu. What had she achieved in her own forty-eight years of life? Nothing to write home about. "I'm very sorry for your loss."

"Thank you. It gets better with time."

"What was she like?"

He looked away, a smile curving his lips. "She was like Martha Stewart. She loved cooking, baking, and entertaining. Nothing made her happier than throwing a meal together and inviting guests to share it."

Reidun winced inside. Why had she asked? Charlotte was the perfect little wife who excelled in homemaking arts. The opposite of her. What did Steinar see in Reidun, then? She was middle-aged in contrast to Charlotte's youth. She thought she looked reasonably good, but setting herself next to Charlotte would be like comparing a wilted cabbage to a rose in full bloom.

Steinar chuckled suddenly. "Look at me, out on a date and all I can talk about is my late wife. I'm sorry."

Reidun forced her facial muscles to return a smile, but her gut twisted. She enjoyed his company, but perhaps it was too early for him to be thinking about finding a new partner. The wound of his loss still seemed to be fresh. "No apology needed," she said. "I wouldn't want you to think you can't talk about Charlotte if you need or want to."

"Thank you. But I don't want you to get the wrong impression." His hand moved closer to hers on the table, and his fingers grazed hers. "I'm thrilled to be out with you and to get to know you better. Charlotte was a precious part of my past, but I'm ready to look ahead."

A delicious tingle trilled from her scalp down to her fingertips as she looked into his gray eyes. "I'm glad to hear that."

He sat back in his chair. "So, how is it that you haven't been on a date in twenty years? I have a good excuse, but I'm not sure you do."

Reidun laughed. "And I'm not sure how to take that."

"Take it as a compliment. From all I've seen and come to know of you, I can't imagine what the male population of Berghaven has been up to all this time."

Heat flushed through her face. "It's really nice of you to say that. Somehow, it's just never happened to me."

He took a sip of water, then fixed his gaze on her. "Oskar told me you and he were engaged."

A chill replaced the flush that had washed over her face. Whose idea was it to be direct tonight? "Yes. Yes, we were. Did he tell you why we broke up?"

"He did, but I'd rather hear it from you."

Reidun's gaze dropped to her hands. "He broke up with me. He didn't think we were compatible. It was hard. I'm not going to lie. It got even harder when he married Elsa less than a year later."

Steinar winced. "Oof."

"Yeah." She let out a mirthless chuckle. "But looking back, it was for the best. He'd just taken over his family business and was deeply involved in making his mark. He wanted me to work with him and be a part of building that legacy. But I wanted to expand in my own trade. Things were finally picking up in my business. We were both working eighty-hour weeks, but toward different goals. I'd worked so hard to get even a shred of respect in my field and I didn't want to give that up."

"Do you regret your choice?"

"I did at first. I even tried to get back together with him, saying I'd give up my business and join him in his, but he turned me down." Her face flooded with heat. Why was she telling Steinar all these embarrassing details? Not even her closest friends knew that she'd gone to Oskar and begged him to give their relationship another chance. "Then I threw myself into my career because it was all I had left. And I avoided dating because I never wanted to have to make the same decision again. I found that men were either freeloaders who wanted me to support them, or hardworking guys who expected me to give up what I was doing and fit in with their lives."

"What about me? Which camp do I fall in?"

Those eyes of his! And these relentless questions. She swallowed. "You're definitely not a freeloader. I don't know if you're the second type."

He shifted in his seat, leaning forward. "Maybe there's a third type. A hardworking man who has room in his life for a strong woman with dreams of her own."

Her throat felt dry, so she gulped a sip of water. "I like that third type."

Steinar opened his mouth to speak, but the waiter approached their table.

"Are you ready to order yet?"

Steinar gritted his teeth at the waiter's intrusion. He stood there with notebook in hand, bobbing and grinning, unaware that he'd just shattered a moment. Steinar blew out a slow breath, letting go of his irritation. They were in a restaurant, after all, and the waiter was only doing his job.

He glanced at Reidun. "Are you ready to order?"

"Not yet."

"Could you give us a bit more time?" He said to the waiter. "We'll let you know when we're ready. Thank you."

The waiter bowed and retreated.

Steinar picked up his menu and tried to make sense of the words. But it was hard to think about food. The connection he felt with Reidun was undeniable. He was deeply attracted to her. How could he fail to be? But that wasn't enough. Not when his children were involved.

And he wasn't sure whether he was right for her, either.

He sensed it had cost her something to be open with him, and now he must do the same. It was time to lay out the pieces of his life face up and let her decide whether she wanted any part of it.

"You just described two types of men. The freeloaders and the ones who expect their women to give up their dreams." He caught and held her gaze. "I'm not going to lie. Perhaps I was that second type before. Twenty years ago, I was probably looking for the same kind of wife that Oskar needed. Someone who would fit her life around my plans. I wouldn't have been able to build my business if Charlotte had wanted to build a big dream of her own. We were perfectly compatible in that way."

Reidun crossed her arms and drew slightly away from the table. "Thanks for being honest."

"I said that was twenty years ago," Steinar said. "I'm not that man anymore. That business I built folded soon after Charlotte passed. My priorities have changed, and I'm in a different place."

Reidun stared at him, her eyes wide. "What do you mean?"

"I started my investment management firm soon after Charlotte and I got married. It was all-consuming, but eventually became very successful. When she got sick, she needed me and the twins were very young. I took time off work and left my business partner in charge." Steinar clenched a fist. "I won't go into all the details unless you want me to, but he made some very ill-advised investments that lost our clients a lot of money. Some of them lost their life savings. It only came to light after Charlotte was gone and I went back to work."

"Oh, no."

"It was a mess, and some of my clients took legal action. I didn't have personal liability, but I felt a moral obligation to make things right with the people who had trusted me. There were some who were facing retirement with no money left. We struck a deal, and I used some of my own savings to repay their losses. It meant I had to sell our home and downsize our lifestyle. Charlotte came from a privileged background and she had expensive tastes. I was happy to give her the standard of living she was used to. But after my company folded, I couldn't afford it anymore. The children's private school, the polo club, that all had to go. I wanted a fresh start without reminders of how much we had lost and away from people who would look down on my children because they were no longer in the same social circle. And so we came here."

He fell silent. Would she think he was a failure? His old friends in England certainly did. And so did his in-laws. They hid it behind whispers and sympathetic looks, but he knew what they were thinking.

Reidun spoke softly. "You said your priorities have changed. What did you mean?"

"My children need me. I can't work one hundred hour weeks and only see them at bedtime. Being present for them is more important than building a multi-million dollar business or shipping them off to exclusive prep schools. I work from home now."

She stared into his eyes. "But is it enough for you? Don't you feel the pull back to fulfill your dream and get the lifestyle you lost?"

Her words took him aback. "I've never thought about that." Did he want to pursue his old dreams? He shook his head, the answer coming to him even as he spoke. "I had my dream job. I built the life I wanted. But I think having what I wanted blinded me from what I needed. Since losing everything, I've come to know my children. Really know them. I wouldn't trade that for all the success I had before. I'm okay with having less stuff if it means making room for the people I love."

Her brown eyes glowed. "So, you're the third type of man."

Warmth flooded his chest. "I hope so. But it's not just about me. I have to think about my children. Have you thought about being involved with someone who has kids?"

A pink tinge touched her tawny cheeks. "It has crossed my mind recently. I think your children are wonderful."

His hand moved across the table. His fingers connected with hers, and he ran his thumb over her velvety soft skin. "I'm very glad to hear that. I want to see where this will go."

"Me too. So does that mean we're going steady?"

Steinar laughed. "Going steady? Do they still call it that?"

"Well, I haven't dated in twenty years. I'm not up on the latest slang." She grinned at him.

"I think twenty years ago, they might have already stopped using that phrase. But, yes, I'm definitely not seeing other people."

"Neither am I. If you—" she broke off as the waiter hovered back beside their table, glancing at them hopefully.

Steinar chuckled. "I think we'd better order. I'll just have the soup of the day followed by—" he ran his finger down the menu and stabbed at a random item. "This. Butter baked trout. And a club soda."

Reidun handed her menu to the waiter. "I'll have what he's having. Thanks."

"Very good monsieur, madame." The waiter scurried away.

Steinar stared at the woman sitting across the table from him. Were they really going to do this? His heart sang.

Was this really happening? Reidun couldn't get over how much she was enjoying this time with Steinar.

They talked about everything. He told her about his childhood, growing up in Hammerfest, and about his father, an oil rig worker who was away for long stretches of time. She learned how stern and distant his father was, expecting nothing short of perfection, and his mother, who did everything right but was emotionally closed. His happiest childhood memories were visiting his grandparents, whose homestead was a few miles outside Berghaven.

"My parents have passed on now," he said. "When I thought about returning to Norway after my time in England, the only place that felt like home was around Berghaven. It never occurred to me to bring Chase and Mya anywhere else."

She told him about growing up with a single father. "I could really relate when Mya told me about sometimes having to go into the stinky men's bathrooms. And it was always really hard to get him a good birthday or Christmas present when I was little because I couldn't go to the store alone."

"I know what you mean," Steinar said. "My birthday is coming up and I've heard Chase and Mya whispering about getting me a gift. Last year their grandmother took them shopping. I really don't mind, but they feel bad if they can't give me something. Especially Mya."

"I wouldn't mind taking them gift shopping. I mean, if it's okay with you."

His eyes lit up with an intensity that went straight to her heart. "Would you? It's really short notice. My birthday is on Thursday next week, so it would have to be before then."

"How about going on Monday? I normally do my bookkeeping in the afternoons, so I can be flexible."

He smiled. "That would be perfect. Their school closes at half-past three."

"Sounds good."

Steinar's phone shrilled, and he frowned while pulling it out of his pocket. "I'm sorry. I set it to silent apart from priority calls." He glanced at the caller ID. "It's the babysitter."

Reidun wrapped her arms around herself. Of course he had to take a call from his babysitter. Karla, their friend

Axel's teenage daughter, was watching the twins tonight.

Reidun watched his face as he took the call.

"Yes, Karla. What?" He frowned, listening. "I see. No, you were absolutely right to call. Would you put her on the line, please?"

Steinar angled his body away so Reidun could no longer see his face. He spoke again into the phone, this time in English, and she could only hear snatches from his end of the conversation. "Hello. This is very unexpected. Your mother said you'd mentioned paying a visit, but she didn't tell me it was decided. I thought you were only thinking about it. No, it's fine. I'll see

you later. Could you put Karla back on, please?"

Reidun frowned. What on earth was going on?

Steinar moved the phone to his other ear. "Hi, Karla. Don't worry. Everything's fine, and I want to stick with our original arrangement. So, yes, please stay until I get back. Thanks. I'll see you soon."

He sighed, stuffing his phone into his pants pocket. He faced Reidun. "Charlotte's sister just arrived on an unexpected visit. She showed up at my doorstep and Karla was worried because she doesn't know her, of course. So Karla called to check with me."

An icy fist tightened around Reidun's gut. "Your sister-in-law is at your house? Do you need to go back now?"

He drummed his fingers on the table for a moment. "For Karla's sake, I think I'd better go. It's probably pretty awkward for her, having someone in the house who's a complete stranger. Karla understands English, of course, but it can't be easy. Do you mind?"

"Of course not."

He smiled, but seemed distracted. "Thank you. I'll call for the check."

Reidun sat back as the waiter produced the check. Something about Steinar's manner made her uneasy. What was this sister-in-law like?

Chapter Fifteen

STEINAR WALKED INTO HIS living room, a chill prickling the back of his neck as he stared at his petite, waif-like sister-in-law. It was like looking into the past. As though Charlotte was living and breathing again.

She sat on the sofa, with her feet drawn up under her. Her short, pale blond hair framed her elfin features, and her deep blue eyes flashed as her gaze collided with his. She beamed at him, a dimple winking in her left cheek. Had Vivian Montague always looked this much like his wife?

She sprang off the sofa and ran toward him. "It's so good to see you. Sorry to just invade your home like this." Her cut-glass accent and melodious voice sounded like an echo of Charlotte's. "I had an offer on my house from someone who wanted a quick sale, and since I haven't found a new place yet, I thought it would be the perfect opportunity to come over and see my lovely niece and nephew. I've missed them so much."

"I'm sure they're delighted to see you, too," he said, stepping away from her. He turned toward Karla, his babysitter. The dark-haired girl was

also on her feet and gathering her things.

"Thanks so much for tonight. Was everything all right with the children?"

Karla nodded. "They were very excited to see their aunt and didn't want to go to bed, but they settled down about an hour ago."

He gave Karla her usual fee in cash.

She tucked the money into her pocket. "Thanks. I'll see myself out."

As she left, Steinar turned to Vivian. "Give me a minute while I check on the children." And while he figured out where she was going to sleep tonight.

All was quiet in the twins' rooms. Both children were fast asleep, in characteristic fashion. Chase had curled up into a ball while Mya lay stretched out like a starfish.

Steinar looked at the space against the wall in Mya's room. Vivian could probably use the same air mattress her mother had used, set up in here.

He went to the hallway closet and reached in the back for the air mattress and pump.

Vivian emerged from the kitchen holding a mug. "I made myself some coffee. Would you like some?"

"No, I'm good. I hope you don't mind a mattress on the floor. You'll sleep in Mya's room."

"That's fine." She went back into the living room and settled back onto the sofa, cradling her mug. "So, were you out with friends?"

He loosened his collar and lowered himself into his armchair. He might as well be upfront. "I was on a date."

"Oh." Her eyebrows flew up. "I wasn't aware that you were seeing someone. But I suppose that's one of the reasons you moved here."

Steinar's ears burned. "Actually, no. We met fairly recently."

"Oh." She blew a stream of air over the drink. "I hope I'll be able to meet her. Are the children aware that you're dating?" She stood and walked over to the bookshelf.

This wasn't any of Vivian's business. He hoped she'd get the point if he avoided her question. He stood, too, and plugged the air pump into a socket. "How are your parents?"

"They're fine. Mummy sends her love, and says you need to confirm your plans for Christmas so she knows when to expect you."

"Oh. Well, we won't be coming for Christmas."

"You won't?" she turned to face him. "Mummy will be disappointed. You know how much she looks forward to spending Christmas with them. She had a lot of plans for the children."

Steinar could guess what Doris's plans involved. A whirlwind of parties and activities, culminating in a stack of presents almost as high as the eight-foot tree. His children would be caught up in the frenzy of piles of expensive stuff. There would be more toys than they could ever play with, more clothes than they could ever wear. It was sweet of Doris to be so generous with her grandchildren, but he wanted them to learn that Christmas was about more than the presents you got. It was one of the few things about which he and Charlotte didn't see eye to eye.

He crossed his arms. "Chase and Mya are looking forward to experiencing a Norwegian Christmas. We're hoping for snow and we're involved in the Christmas fair, too."

"That sounds exciting. You seem to be settling in very well here. Taking part in the Christmas fair, dating." She straightened a portrait of Charlotte on the bookshelf. "I even heard the children saying things to that babysitter in Norwegian."

"It's starting to feel like home. We're working hard to settle in."

"I'm looking forward to getting to know the place. You'll have to show me around soon."

Steinar brought the mattress to the pump. "It's late, and we have church tomorrow. I'll set this up so you can get some sleep."

The noise of the pump drowned out any immediate response from her. While it filled up the mattress, he went to the linen closet and grabbed a duvet, pillow, and bedsheets.

Vivian reached for the bed linen as he headed to Mya's room. "Don't worry about that. I'll sort myself out. Sure you don't want to have a drink?"

He shook his head. "No, I'm tired. Church starts at half-past nine, so we'll leave around quarter past. Good night."

She waggled her fingers at him. Another trick of Charlotte's. "Good night."

He went into his bedroom and closed the door behind him.

Lowering himself onto his bed, he pulled out his cell phone. Was it too late to send Reidun a text?

He typed in his message app.

I had a wonderful time tonight. Looking forward to seeing you again.

He sent the message and waited a couple of minutes for a reply, but none came. She was probably asleep. He'd see her tomorrow.

Reidun buzzed with excitement as she prepared to leave for church. She'd woken up to find a sweet text message from Steinar and sent back a reply. He didn't text her back, but he was probably getting the children ready, and she was going to see him in a few minutes.

She chose her favorite pair of slacks, a dove gray color that went with anything, and paired them with a lilac sweater. Picking up two pairs of earrings, she scrutinized the effect of both choices. She decided on the demure pearl ones, then picked up a hairbrush.

Perhaps they could spend the afternoon together. Go for a nice walk with the children and then have dinner. He hadn't mentioned whether he would bring his sister-in-law to church. If she came, should Reidun introduce herself?

She paused, with her brush halfway to her hair. Maybe it was too soon to be meeting each other's families. She wasn't sure how to play it, but she'd follow Steinar's lead.

She got to church just before the service started. Steinar and his family didn't seem to be there.

As the first hymn began, she glanced up to see Steinar and the twins walking along the aisle, heading to their usual seats. Reidun's heart stuttered. That woman walking between Chase and Mya. It was as though Charlotte had stepped out of the portrait on Steinar's wall and was walking in Bethel Church, wearing an elegant pleated skirt and silk blouse. She was young, gorgeous, and bore an unmistakable resemblance to the children.

Reidun's heart hammered. The sister-in-law. What did Steinar say her name was? Veronica? She couldn't tear her gaze away as they settled into their seats, looking just like a family. Her gut churned as Mya strained up-

ward to whisper something into her aunt's ear. The woman answered, her face dimpling in a smile.

Seated together, they looked like a perfect matched set. Steinar, Chase, Mya, and Charlotte 2.0 or whatever her name was.

Reidun joined belatedly in the hymn with the rest of the congregation. Everything would be okay. There was nothing to worry about. So what if Steinar's late wife had a look-alike sister who was staying with him? Steinar had known this woman for years, but Reidun was the one he was dating now.

She avoided looking their way for the rest of the service.

When it ended, she stayed in her seat. If Steinar wanted to introduce her to his sister-in-law, he would come and find her. She wouldn't approach them.

She sensed him next to her before she saw him and raised her gaze to look at his face.

"Hi," he said. "I—"

"There you are, Steinar," a voice behind him said in English.

He turned his head and spoke in the same language. "Vivian, this is my... my friend, Reidun. Reidun, my sister-in-law Vivian."

Friend, was it? Okay. She squashed the tendril of disappointment that coiled around her heart. She'd told herself she would play it by ear, following his lead about how he wanted to introduce her to his family.

Reidun stood and shook the hand Vivian held out. The younger woman was even more stunning up close, her flawless skin enhanced with only minimal makeup. "Glad to meet you," Reidun said.

She stole a glance at Vivian's other hand. No rings.

Vivian's gaze swept over Reidun like a scanning beacon. "The pleasure's all mine. It's lovely to be here. I didn't follow the service, of course, but it was nice to hear some familiar songs."

"Familiar? So, you go to church in England?"

"Yes. I'm a regular at St. Margaret's, where Steinar and my sister used to go."

"Have you been in Norway before?" Reidun asked.

"I've been to Oslo and Bergen with my sister. This is my first time coming so far north. I'm hoping to get a glimpse of the northern lights."

"You've come at the right time of the year," Reidun said. "We'll soon be going into *mørketiden*, the dark time, when the sun won't rise again until January. You should have a good chance of seeing the northern lights."

"How on earth can you stand it being dark for so long? It's bad enough in England when the sun sets at around four."

Reidun shrugged. "I grew up here, so it's all I've ever known. And it helps that Christmas comes at around the darkest time, so all the decorations and lights make everything look much more cheerful and cozy. When there's snow it's even better."

Vivian glanced at Steinar. "I guess that must be part of the charm of a Norwegian Christmas."

"Yes," he said. "And I want the children to experience it. Speaking of Chase and Mya, I'd better round them up." He walked away, leaving the two women.

Reidun had a lot of questions for Vivian, none of which were appropriate. Like how long are you staying? Why did you show up out of the blue? What exactly is the relationship between you and Steinar?

She finally landed on something suitable to ask. "Did you see much of Steinar and the children when they lived in England?"

Vivian beamed. "Oh, yes. My sister and I were very close. I was always in and out of their home, and the children would often stay with me overnight when Steinar and Charlotte wanted some private husband and wife time."

Steinar came up with the children as Vivian was still talking. Reidun's face was on fire. Had he heard what Vivian said?

Mya slipped her hand into her aunt's.

Vivian looked up at Steinar. "I'm a bit worried about that pot roast. I'm not entirely sure how your oven cooks, so I want to check on it."

Steinar nodded and turned to Reidun. "I'll call you later."

She watched them walk away, feeling like an outsider looking at the perfect family unit.

"Who was that?"

Reidun turned to see Bethany, whose gaze also followed the Jakobsens. "Steinar's sister-in-law is visiting."

"They seem cozy. Do you think there's anything going on between them?"

Reidun swallowed. "What makes you think that?"

Bethany's eyes twinkled. "I know a thing or two about marrying brothers-in-law."

Reidun's heart plummeted. Bethany had lost her husband several years earlier and recently married his older brother, a man who had loved her in secret for a long time. And she thought something like that might be going on with Steinar and Vivian?

"Aw, look at them," Bethany said. "They make such a cute couple."

Reidun started to say that she and Steinar had actually started dating, but the words lodged in her throat.

Bethany was one of her closest friends, and they'd been working on the Christmas fair committee for some time now. If her best friend couldn't picture her and Steinar to-gether but started speculating about Vivian the instant she'd seen her, what did that say? Was Reidun such a strange and outlandish choice for Steinar?

Steinar clenched his fists as he walked across the church parking lot. Why had he said Reidun was just his friend?

Maybe he should have told Vivian straight out that Reidun was the woman he was dating.

But Chase and Mya didn't know. This relationship was still so new. He wanted to sit down with them and have a proper conversation about it when the time was right, and not have them just overhear something this important.

He unlocked the car doors, and the children jumped into the back seat.

Vivian took a step toward the driver's seat and giggled. "Oops! I'm sorry. The passenger seat is on the other side here, isn't it? I'm so used to right hand drive cars."

Steinar forced a smile as she walked around to the other side of the car.

Vivian's visit couldn't have come at a worse time. He, Reidun, and the children needed time and space to be together and let what was between them grow naturally, without scrutiny and comment from outsiders.

And Vivian was an outsider.

He got into the driver's seat. He was going to need to pray about all of this. A lot.

Chapter Sixteen

ON MONDAY MORNING STEINAR and his children sat at the breakfast table while Vivian flipped over a slice of French toast.

She slid it onto a plate, added a couple of pieces of bacon, and set the dish in front of Steinar. "There you go."

"Thanks." He normally made do with a bowl of muesli, so having a cooked breakfast was a treat.

He looked at his children as they ate, then watched Vivian wipe down the counter. The scene was familiar

and yet discordant, as though he were playing a piece on the piano with the correct rhythm but with his fingers on the wrong keys.

He bit into a rasher of bacon. Vivian made it exactly how Charlotte did, just the way he liked it. Crispy and piping hot.

She sat in the chair opposite him. "I thought it would be fun to walk the children to school today."

"Yes!" Mya grinned around a mouthful of French toast. "And you can get us again in the afternoon."

"You're supposed to go to the mall with Reidun after school," Steinar said. Reidun was taking them to pick up a birthday present for him, and he knew how much she was looking forward to hanging out with them. It was part of the process of easing her into their lives.

Chase brightened. "Awesome! But can't Aunt Vivian come, too?"

Vivian dabbed her lips with a napkin. "This is the Reidun we met at church? Your... um... friend? I'd hate to intrude if they had plans with her."

He could see the wheels turning in her head. Vivian was smart. She'd probably put two and two together and figured out that Reidun was the woman he was dating. It wasn't a secret, but he wanted to make sure his children found out from him.

Steinar pushed his plate away, his breakfast half-eaten. Would it be rude to ask Reidun to include Vivian? Perhaps it would be even more impolite and awkward to tell Vivian she couldn't go. He clenched and un-clenched his fist. "It'll probably be okay, but I'll give her a heads-up."

"Yay," Mya said.

Vivian leaned toward Chase and ruffled his blond hair. "This is getting way too long. Your mother loved you to look tidy. Maybe we should stop by the barber's and get you a trim."

Chase shook his head. "I like it like this."

"Yeah, he's growing it so he can look like Link," Mya said.

Vivian frowned. "Link?"

"You know," Chase said. "Link, the hero from the *Legend of Zelda*."

"Oh, is that a movie?" Vivian asked.

"It's a video game. Or a series of video games," Chase said. "Reidun knows. She one hundred percented *Breath of the Wild* in Master Mode and *Skyward Sword* in Hard Mode."

"Oh, I see. Video games were never really my thing." Vivian took a sip of her coffee and stood. "Shouldn't we be off? Finish your breakfast and brush your teeth, children, while I put your lunch boxes in your bags. Let's see if I've got it right. This lovely pink one must belong to Chase and Mya's is the one with pirates on it?"

"No!" the children yelled in chorus.

There was a bustle of activity and, as if by magic, the table was cleared and the children stood at the door, ready to leave.

Vivian pulled on her coat. "Let's go. Say bye to Dad."

"Bye, Dad," the children echoed. They left, plunging the house into silence, although noise still clanged in Steinar's head.

He picked up his phone and dialed Reidun's number.

Her voice swept over him like a soothing breeze. "Hi, Steinar. How are Chase and Mya?"

"They're fine. Charlotte walked them to school. I mean Vivian." His face burned as he caught himself mixing up his wife and sister-in-law's names.

Reidun was silent for several heartbeats. Then she said, "That's very helpful for you."

"It is. Are you still good to take them to the mall this afternoon?"

"I'm looking forward to it."

"Do you mind if Vivian tags along? She doesn't have any other plans this afternoon and the children are keen to spend time with her. Um, with both of you. They definitely want to hang out with you." Why couldn't he say anything right today?

"Oh. Yes, yes, of course. I'll pick them up at four. Is it okay if I get the children a snack?"

"That would be good. They're usually hungry after school. And I'll make dinner for all of us." He hesitated for a moment, not sure how to put his thoughts into words. "Reidun, it's been a bit strange since we went out. I haven't really had time to catch my breath and settle into..." he trailed off, words defying him.

"I think I get what you're trying to say. Do you want to... to hold back from seeing each other for a while?"

"No!" He clenched a fist. He was making a complete mess of this. "No, that's not what I'm trying to say. Not at all. I just wanted to ease into this new phase with the children, but Vivian being here makes it hard."

Then it hit him. Vivian made him feel as though he was betraying Charlotte's memory. She reminded him so much of his late wife. What if she had the same effect on his children? The timing of her arrival was uncanny. But he couldn't tell Reidun that. He needed to work through his irrational feelings before he hurt her.

He sighed. "I just wish we had some time to talk about this. The children don't know that I'm seeing you yet, and I want to tell them myself."

"I understand."

Did she, though?

She went on, "Do they have a budget they need to stick to? For your birthday present, I mean. Just so I know what kind of stores to look into."

"They'll be using money from their allowance, so please don't let them spend more than about a hundred kroner each. Fifty would be even better."

He was glad she'd brought up the

practical side of things. It had slipped his mind.

"Okay. I'm sure we can get you a hideous tie or some questionable socks for that."

He chuckled. "Sounds good. I'm sure I'll be delighted. Thanks again for doing this."

"That's okay. See you later."

Steinar ended the call, then settled at his desk to start his work. It was illogical for him to feel so uneasy. What had really changed since two days ago? He'd had a lovely date with Reidun, they'd become a couple, and then his sister-in-law arrived. Vivian's presence changed nothing, and he needed to shake this crazy feeling of foreboding.

Chapter Seventeen

REIDUN TRAILED BEHIND VIVIAN and the twins in the Berghaven Mall, loaded with shopping bags and the children's school backpacks. So much for bonding with Chase and Mya on this shopping trip.

Vivian was in full charge of the outing and Reidun was relegated to bag carrier and occasional interpreter.

She'd given up trying to follow the conversation as they chattered in rapid-fire English, full of what she sensed were inside jokes that someone who wasn't part of the family wouldn't get even if they were a native speaker of the language.

Vivian paused in front of a menswear boutique. "What do you think, kids? Shall we look in here? This looks like the kind of place we might find something for your dad."

The younger woman walked into the store.

Reidun followed. This was a high-end store, and the prices were likely to be way beyond the children's budget. But there was a sale rack which promised some deep discounts.

Reidun pointed to a display of items on clearance. "Maybe your father would like a nice necktie?"

"Hm, I'm not sure," Vivian said while the children came over to the rack. "Steinar is very picky about the kinds of ties he wears, and I don't know whether any of these are suitable."

Reidun touched a silvery gray tie with a paisley pattern. At fifty percent off, it was just barely within the budget. "This is a nice one. What do you think, Chase? Do you think your dad would like this?"

The boy looked at his aunt.

Vivian tilted her head. "I'm not sure about any of these. Let's keep looking." She glanced up at Reidun. "When you've known someone as long as I've known Steinar, you get a definite sense of what their taste is. When did you first meet him, again?"

Reidun's face burned. "About three months ago."

"Not any longer than that?" Vivian's blue eyes widened. She stared at Reidun for a long, wordless moment.

Reidun got the message. Vivian had a long shared history with Steinar and the twins that Reidun couldn't come close to matching.

Vivian turned away from the ties. "Oh, look over there. I see some really nice wallets."

They walked to the display rack.

Reidun's eyebrows flew up at the prices. The cheapest was around four hundred kroner. She leaned toward Vivian and spoke in a low voice so the children wouldn't hear. "Steinar told me he didn't want the children spending more than one hundred kroner each on his present."

Vivian brushed Reidun's comment away with an airy wave of her delicate hand. "Oh, that's not a problem at all," she said in her clear, bell-like tone. "I can make up the shortfall. They need to get their father something nice. I think this one over here is perfect."

She picked up a tan-colored leather billfold that cost just under six hundred kroner. "I think your dad would love this. What do you think, Chase? Shall we get it?"

Reidun bit her tongue as Chase nodded enthusiastically.

"What about me?" Mya said. "I need to get a present for him, too."

Vivian put the wallet into the shopping basket. "What about an aftershave? They have some over there, and I know exactly the one your dad likes."

Vivian chose a bottle that cost almost seven times Steinar's approved budget.

A queasiness settled in Reidun's gut. She had to reason with Vivian. She spoke quietly. "Vivian, Steinar was very clear. He said they shouldn't spend more than one hundred kroner, and fifty would be better."

A glint of steel entered Vivian's voice. "I said I've got this. There's no need to pinch pennies."

Reidun let it go. Arguing in front of the children would be worse than spending a few more kroner than planned.

They left the store, Vivian holding the cute little carrier bag over her wrist. "That was a good afternoon's work." She gasped as she caught sight of a nail shop. "Oh, look! Perfect. I really need to get my nails done. They look absolutely shocking." She glanced at Reidun. "Do you mind?"

"No, not at all," Reidun said. She avoided looking at her own hands. "About how long do you think you'll be?"

Vivian shrugged. "I'll just get a basic one. So, maybe half an hour? They don't look too busy."

Reidun glanced at her watch. "Okay. We'll pop into the bookstore first and then the toy store. Are you okay with that, children?"

The twins nodded eagerly.

Vivian waved a hand. "See you in half an hour, then."

Reidun put down the bags and sank gratefully into the comfortable armchair at the bookstore. This was one of those wonderful places that believed in giving the customers cozy reading nooks. She turned to the children. "Why don't you browse what you want, and I'll sit right here and wait for you? Stay where I can see you."

"Okay," the twins said in chorus.

Reidun grabbed the chance to check her phone for messages. Her senior plumbing supervisor had sent her two texts, asking about whether he was authorized to buy an expensive part needed for a repair job.

She exchanged a couple more texts with him, then glanced at her email.

The children. She looked up suddenly. They'd been browsing the shelf just opposite her, but she couldn't see them anymore.

She jumped to her feet, scanning the aisle. Maybe they went to the next one over.

She walked up and down the next two aisles, her heart rate escalating with each step. There was no sign of Chase and Mya.

Reidun's gaze bounced around the store. There were two floors: one above and the other beneath this one. Where could they be? She'd only looked at her phone for a few minutes.

She ran up to a woman in the store uniform who was slotting books onto a shelf. "Excuse me, did you see a boy and a girl aged about seven standing around here? They have blond hair and are about this tall."

The woman nodded. "Yeah, I did. Some minutes ago."

"Do you know where they went?"

The woman shook her head apologetically. "Sorry, I didn't really pay attention. Are they missing?"

"Yes. I can't see them."

"Okay, well, just remain calm. We'll do our best to find them. I'll get my manager."

The girl was back a minute later, walking briskly toward Reidun with an older woman in a dark blue suit and a name tag that said "Signy."

Signy spoke quickly, pulling out a tablet. "Hello. I understand you're missing your children. Can you let me know their names and physical descriptions?"

Reidun took a deep breath and focused on speaking coherently. "The girl is Mya Jakobsen. She's got blue eyes and long wavy blond hair in a ponytail with one of those big clip-on bows. She's wearing a purple puffy jacket, blue jeans, and purple sneakers. The boy is wearing a blue puffy jacket, blue jeans, and white sneakers.

He's also got blond wavy hair and blue eyes. His name is Chase Jakobsen."

Signy tapped quickly on her tablet with a stylus. "Don't worry—I'm sure we'll find them. We have a missing child protocol and we're doing everything we can. Wait here, please."

The woman hurried away while Reidun stood frozen in place, her heart hammering.

Her phone rang and she jerked it out of her pocket with stiff fingers. It was Steinar.

Chapter Eighteen

STEINAR STOOD FROZEN TO the spot, his phone pressed to his ear. "What do you mean, the children are missing?"

"I—they were right here browsing the books in the aisle." The edge of panic in Reidun's voice sent his pulse skyrocketing. "I checked my phone for just a few minutes, and when I looked up, they were gone."

"Have you called the police? Where are you?"

Her voice shook. "I'm at the Book Basket in Berghaven Mall. They told me they have a missing child protocol that they're following. They'll tell me if—when—to call the police."

Steinar spoke over her. "I'm on my way."

He stuffed his phone into his pocket and grabbed his keys on the way out the door. *God, please keep my children safe.*

What would he do if something happened to them? And how could they disappear when Reidun and Vivian were with them?

He jumped into his car and peeled off his driveway, forcing an approaching vehicle to swerve out of his way.

The prayer cycled through his head. *God, please keep my children safe. Please keep them safe.* What could Reidun and Vivian have been doing to let the children out of their sight?

He made the ten-minute trip to the mall in just over six minutes, parking askew across two spaces. He burst out of the car and sprinted to the entrance of the mall. *Dear Lord, watch over my children.*

Steinar elbowed his way past slower-moving shoppers. The blue and white lettering of the Book Basket loomed ahead, and Steinar barreled toward it.

"Sorry," he mumbled as he bumped into a woman carrying a load of shopping.

"Excuse me," she screeched. "How rude!"

"I said I'm sorry, okay?" he snapped. "What else do you want?" He turned his back on the seething woman and plowed on ahead. He didn't have time for this. His children were lost.

He rushed into the Book Basket just as a voice spoke on the public announcement system.

"This is a customer announcement. Would Mya Jakobsen and Chase Jakobsen please come to the children's section. Mya and Chase Jakobsen are urgently requested to come to the children's section."

He clenched his fists. The fools were making the announcement in Norwegian. Even if his children heard it, they probably wouldn't understand.

A man built like a brick wall barred Steinar's way. "Excuse me, sir. We're having a security situation and aren't letting customers in. Sincere apologies, but I have to ask you to wait outside."

"It's my children. My children Mya and Chase are the ones who are missing."

The security guard blinked at him. "Oh. Oh, okay. I'm sorry. Please go over to the children's section over that way and speak to the manager. She's called the missing child protocol and will tell you what to do."

Steinar ran toward the back of the store while the man was still speaking. A knot of people stood together. Reidun's tall figure was among them.

Her eyes were red and tear-filled as she looked toward him. "Steinar, I—"

"What's going on?" He brushed past Reidun's outstretched hand, pivoting toward the woman in a business-suit who stood next to her. "Are you in charge? I'm the children's father. What's happening?"

The woman glanced at Reidun as though to confirm Steinar's words. He held back his annoyance as the woman faced him again.

"I'm the on-duty manager. We have a very robust missing child protocol and everything is being done to locate your children."

"Everything? Have you called the police?"

"Things haven't quite reached that stage yet."

"What are you waiting for? For someone to drive off with them?" His voice rose. "I don't care about your protocol. I'm calling the police now."

"Sir, if you would just wait a couple of minutes. This protocol was worked out with the police. We're searching for the children on every floor. As soon as we establish they're not on the premises, we'll call the police. Sometimes the child is in the bathroom or in an out of the way corner. The police will want to make sure we've completed this search."

Her logic penetrated the red fog of his panic. He held up his finger. "One minute. Then I'm calling the police, whatever your protocol says."

He turned away from the manager and pushed a hand through his hair, his gaze landing on Reidun.

Tears streaming down her face, she stood with her arms wrapped tightly against her mid-section.

"Reidun, what happened? You were supposed to be watching them. And where's Vivian?"

She wrung her hands. "Vivian didn't come here with us. She's in the nail shop. I was here with Chase and Mya, and they were standing at that shelf looking at the Pokémon books. I checked my work messages for just a minute or two and when I looked up, they were gone."

White hot rage seared his chest. "Are you sure it was just a minute or two?"

"I can't be sure exactly how long it was, but it wasn't more than that."

"It must have been longer than that if they managed to find their way out of the store. Do you have any idea how dangerous that was? Are you so utterly clueless about what might happen to them? How can you lose two children?" He stepped toward her, his hands balling into fists.

Reidun flinched, backing into a rotating book display. "I'm so sorry," she whispered. "It really was just a minute."

"If you'd had any experience with kids, you'd know that a lot can happen in just a minute. I trusted you with my children, Reidun. My children." His shout snapped in the air like a whip.

Her face crumpled, and he spun away.

The manager stared at him, her lips in a tight line.

He pulled out his phone. "Your minute is up. I'm calling the police now."

She didn't try to stop him as he punched the emergency digits into the keypad.

"Look! They're—they're over there," Reidun said, her voice choked. "Thank God!"

Steinar whipped around to look where she was pointing.

Chase and Mya walked toward them, Vivian holding each child by the hand.

Steinar ran forward and pulled his children into his arms. "Where have you been? We were all so worried about you."

Vivian's voice rang out. "What's going on? Nobody will explain anything to me."

Steinar stood, an arm around each child. "The children went missing from the store. I was just about to call the police. But what happened? Did you find them?"

Vivian frowned. "Find them? They were with me. I took them to get smoothies. Why did you think they were missing?"

"You took them?" He stared at her.

"Yes. I decided to skip the full manicure because the technician was so clumsy with the massage. When I came in here and saw the children, I asked them whether they wanted a drink, and we went to get one."

A chill started in his core. "You didn't tell Reidun you were taking them."

The store supervisor spoke. "I'm glad to see the children are safe. If you'll excuse me, I'll be going now."

Steinar's face burned. "Thank you. I'm very sorry about earlier. I probably sounded very rude."

"No apology necessary for me, at least. I'm a parent myself, and I know how anxious you were. I'm just happy the children were found." She nodded toward Reidun and walked away.

Reidun stood apart from the group, gripping the back of a chair, her head bowed. The shaking fingers of her other hand covered her mouth.

Merciful heaven, the things he'd said to her—what had he done?

Steinar turned toward Vivian, his throat dry. "Would you mind taking the children to the toy store or something? I'll meet you there."

"Yay!" Mya dropped his hand. "Let's go, Aunt Vivian."

He watched his children and Vivian walk away, then turned to face Reidun. "Can we talk?"

Reidun's whole body shook as she watched Vivian lead the children away. They were safe. Thank God. But they'd been with their aunt this whole time?

"Can we talk?" Steinar asked.

Her legs wouldn't hold her up. She sank into the nearest chair. It was made for children and not an adult-sized person, never mind a tall one. Her long legs bent awkwardly.

Steinar sat opposite her, moving slowly as he lowered his large frame into the ridiculously tiny chair.

"Reidun, I'm so sorry." His voice was raw.

She pulled away as his fingertips brushed hers. No matter how sorry he was, he couldn't unring the bell. Something had broken in those past few minutes, and she needed to figure out what it was.

"I..." She swallowed. "I was on my phone. I should have noticed them leave. They walked away with Vivian, but it might have been a stranger."

"They wouldn't have just gone off with a stranger, though," he said. "They left so quickly because it was someone they knew. I should never have spoken to you the way I did. And I shouldn't have shouted at you."

An unbearable ache weighed on her chest. She spoke slowly, groping for words to express the thoughts churning in her mind. "What's bothering me most is you said this wouldn't have happened if I was better at looking after children."

"I'm sorry." He pleaded with his hands. "I was panicking and not thinking straight. All that was in my mind was finding Chase and Mya."

"I know. I was terrified, too. But doesn't it tell you something that your first assumption was that I'd done something wrong?"

"I thought I'd lost my children. Are you really going to judge me by my impulse behavior on my worst day? Based on things I said in a blind panic before I'd even had a chance to think?"

"That's just it," she said. "That was your gut reaction, with no filter to soften what you really believe. Deep down, you don't trust me."

"Of course I trust you. I wouldn't have asked you to take them out if I didn't."

She weighed his words. His apologies, the plea in his eyes. But his earlier words hung heavier. *Are you so utterly clueless about what might happen to them? How can you lose two children?* She saw his face, contorted with rage as he shouted at her. He'd looked at her as though he hated her.

Her heart shattered. Would she ever get that image out of her head?

Pushing away from the low table, she got to her feet.

Steinar stood as well, his gaze still locked on her face. "Reidun, please forgive me."

She looked away from him, toward the jumble of bags next to the table. The children's school backpacks lay alongside the shopping bags.

She picked up her purse. "Those are the children's things."

"Please, Reidun." He gripped her arm.

She looked into his face, at the moisture in his gray eyes.

"I'm sorry," he said.

She swallowed past the agonizing ache in her throat. "I know I need to forgive you, but I need time. Can you understand that? I can't just sweep this under the rug."

He drew in a ragged breath. "Okay. I understand."

Tears filling her eyes, she pulled the strap of her purse over her shoulder. "I'm going home."

Chapter Nineteen

STEINAR RIPPED A PARKING ticket off the windshield of his double-parked car as Vivian and the children got into their seats.

Wonderful. Now he had to pay a fine on top of everything else today.

He got into the car and slammed the door. Why had he been such an idiot?

Vivian opened her mouth as if to speak, then scanned his face and said nothing.

Good. He didn't want to hear anything she had to say. She'd been a thorn in his side from the moment she showed up here in Berghaven. She'd ruined his date with Reidun, and now, by her thoughtless actions, she might have destroyed his fledgling relationship before it even got off the ground.

He gritted his teeth as he steered the car along the road home.

Thanks to Vivian, Reidun had gone through the agony of thinking Chase and Mya had gone missing under her watch. He'd shouted at her and crushed her with his words. None of it would have happened if Vivian had taken ten seconds to tell Reidun she was taking the twins. And now he might have lost the woman who was finally waking up his heart. He wanted to scream out his rage and

frustration. But he couldn't. Not in front of the children.

In the house, the ingredients for a stir fry lay half-chopped where he'd left them on the kitchen counter.

His stomach rebelled against the idea of food, but Chase and Mya needed to eat. He turned and spoke to them. "Could you go to your rooms and play video games or something? I'll call you out for dinner."

"Are you mad at us?" Chase asked.

Steinar took a moment to draw a slow breath. "No, I'm not mad at you. I just need to be quiet for some time."

Wide-eyed, the children exchanged glances and left quietly.

Steinar washed his hands, grabbed a knife, and attacked the ingredients on the counter.

Vivian followed him into the kitchen. *Lord, give me strength.* Couldn't she give him some space?

Gritting his teeth, he brought his knife down on a pile of bok choi.

Vivian sat on a chair at the kitchen table. "Is everything okay with Reidun?"

"No." He swiped the vegetables with a vicious slash. "She's devastated. She thought the children had gone missing, and that it was her fault."

"I'm sorry," Vivian said. "When I came to the bookshop, I thought she'd seen me waving at the children to come with me. I didn't realize she hadn't noticed us leaving. Perhaps I imagined she was more attentive. I should have made sure she'd seen me before we left. I agree that was on me, but I thought she was watching them."

Steinar shook his head. She was still insinuating that Reidun did something wrong? He wanted to be angry with Vivian. Anger was the easy way out. It would be a relief to pile all the blame on her head. Making it someone else's fault would take the load off his own shoulders. But the painful truth was, Vivian hadn't hurt Reidun. He, Steinar, had done that all on his own.

He sighed, turning back to the vegetables. Instead of reaching out to Reidun and coming together in a tough time, he'd turned on her and ripped her to shreds. She was right to pull away from him.

The knife slipped, narrowly missing the tip of his thumb.

Vivian held out a hand. "You'd better put that knife down before you lose a finger. I'll finish making dinner."

He didn't object, handing the knife to her.

She took it from him, positioning herself in front of the chopping board. "A stir fry, right?"

"Yes."

She grabbed a bunch of spring onions from the pile of washed vegetables.

He sat in a chair, watching her as she worked. She would have a perfect

meal whipped up in minutes. Even her hands were just like Charlotte's. Small, delicate and doll-like, her fingernails like pearl-tipped ovals.

Why hadn't he fallen for Vivian? He sometimes got the feeling that's what her mother wanted.

He'd known Vivian for years. She was charming and smart, and as beautiful as her sister. After Charlotte's death, Vivian had been a constant presence, helping him and the twins.

He thought of another pair of hands. Strong, capable, and brown, holding a towing strap, doing card tricks, and repairing a leaking toilet.

He didn't need another Charlotte. He wanted Reidun. Now that she'd pushed him away, he was more certain than ever. How would he convince her of that?

The cold nipped at Steinar's fingers and he shoved his hands deeper into his pockets as he strode along the sidewalk of a residential street later that evening. It was always easier to pray and think when he was outside.

His children were asleep at home, with Vivian still in the house. He desperately needed this time to work through the events of the afternoon. It didn't matter where he walked. Just the act of moving made it easier to pray.

An icy blast of wind hit his face. Winter came early here in the far north. Although still mid-November, it was already colder than it ever got in England. He'd need to get warmer clothes for himself and the twins as soon as possible. Long undergarments, thicker socks, snow boots, lots of things they could layer up.

That meant a trip to the mall. He sighed. The mall. He'd messed up so badly this afternoon. Barging into that woman and then being rude to her. Not to mention the way he'd spoken to the store manager who was doing what she could to find his children.

And then there was Reidun.

His face heated against the wintry air as his words to her came back to him. *Lord, forgive my callous and cutting words.*

And he wasn't just a clod-headed idiot. He was a hypocrite, too. He couldn't swear that he kept an eagle eye on the twins every second when they were out.

Just a few months ago, when he fell asleep at the wheel, he'd put them in more danger than Reidun ever had. He'd been lucky that they only ended up in a ditch.

And Reidun had rescued them.

A fresh pang of anguish seared his gut. Could he blame her for being upset with him? His angry outburst had probably waved every red flag into her face. If only there was a way to show her how deeply he regretted his actions and how much he valued her.

Things had moved fast with Reidun. Maybe too fast. They'd had no time to find their footing, and now their relationship was hurtling over a cliff. Would they be able to save it?

"Steinar. Is that you?"

He spun around. Bethany, one of the members of the Christmas fair committee, stood at the end of a driveway a few feet away, holding a wheelie bin.

"Oh, hi, Bethany. Taking out the trash?"

"Yes. What are you doing around our neck of the woods? At first, I thought you might be dropping in for a visit, but you walked right past me."

He looked around, taking in the neighborhood he was in. He hadn't realized he'd walked this far from home. "I didn't see you there. I needed a breath of fresh air."

"Everything okay with the children?"

"Yes, they're fine. I left them at home with their aunt. I guess I'd better head back."

She tilted her head, smiling. "Must be nice having your sister-in-law around to help. Lukas and I would love to have the two of you over for a meal sometime. With the children, of course," she added.

"Thanks," Steinar said. He was half-way turned to leave when the tone of her words struck him. He faced her again. "Wait. You don't think Vivian and I are an item, do you?"

"Oh. Um..." she looked flustered. "I just assumed... you mean you're not?"

"No. Not in the least."

"I see." She shifted her weight from one foot to the other. "Sorry about that. Well, this is awkward. I thought, being your late wife's sister, and such a lovely person, it made sense for you to—"

Without knowing why, he blurted out, "It's Reidun I'm interested in. We've just started dating."

Her jaw dropped. "Really? You and Reidun? She never told me."

"It hasn't been long. But why does that seem so strange?"

"It's just that I would never have put the two of you together." Frowning, she put her finger on her cheek. "But when I think about it, I can see how it would work. Like avocado and coffee."

He gave her a double take. "What?"

"Avocado and coffee. You know, they're both delicious on their own and with other completely different things, but you'd never imagine they'd go together. We have a friend who has a food blog. She's always making interesting stuff, and once she was telling us about how you could make this amazing milkshake with avocado and coffee. We didn't believe her, but she made one for us and it was incredible. Mindblowingly good. Reidun says it's her favorite milkshake ever."

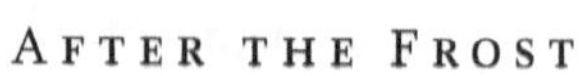

"I see."

"So, yeah. Two things that you don't automatically put together can actually work." She winced. "But I opened my big mouth the other day and told Reidun I thought you and Vivian would be a cute couple. I'm sorry."

Steinar sighed. Could this mess get any more tangled? "It's not exactly smooth sailing."

He told her the brief history of his romance with Reidun, including what had happened that afternoon.

As he finished talking, the front door opened behind Bethany and her husband peeked out.

She waved. "Hey sweetheart. I ran into Steinar and we just got to talking."

"You've been out so long I was about to send a search party," Lukas said. "Hi, Steinar. Why don't you come in and have some coffee? It's freezing out here."

Steinar wanted to stay. Talking about Reidun was the next best thing to being with her. But he reluctantly shook his head.

"I appreciate your offer, but I'd better go back home and unravel some of the mess I'm in." He looked first at Bethany, then at Lukas. "Please pray for me."

She squeezed his arm. "We will. And don't give up."

Chapter Twenty

REIDUN CAUGHT A GLIMPSE of herself in the dark kitchen window. What a perfect reflection of her life. A middle-aged woman hunched alone over a TV dinner.

Why had she met Steinar? Why did she allow herself to hope for something more? What would the man who'd had Charlotte as a wife want with her?

Perhaps in a moment of weakness and loneliness he'd deluded himself into thinking they could have a future. He'd spread that delusion to her, too.

But Vivian showed up and slotted so perfectly into his life, reminding Reidun of what kind of woman Steinar had chosen to build a family with. And even without Vivian, his words at the bookstore were proof of how he really saw Reidun.

Lord, what did I do wrong? What should I have done differently?

She dumped her half-eaten dinner in the trash and rummaged in the freezer for a tub of ice cream. If she was going to have a pity party, she might as well do it right.

Had she learned nothing from her entanglement with Oskar? Sometimes, two people just didn't belong together.

And that was another layer of misery to add to the pile. When she and Oskar had broken up, her friends were there to rally around her.

Now, she couldn't even count on that. They were so busy with their lives that they didn't even know what was going on with her.

She spooned a scoop of salted caramel ice cream into her mouth.

Tomorrow, she would be strong and pick up the threads of her life. Tonight, though, she wanted to wallow for a while.

Her doorbell rang, causing her heart to leap in her chest. It was well after eleven at night. Who on earth was it?

She went to the front hallway and peered through the peephole. Bethany?

She opened the door. Not just Bethany but Sonia, Lisa, and even Johanna, who was supposed to be in Trondheim. All her best friends. "What's going on? What are you all doing here?"

She moved aside, and the women crowded into the hallway.

Bethany said, "I ran into Steinar tonight, and he told me everything. And I couldn't believe all that had been going on and I—we—didn't know."

A painful lump clogged Reidun's throat.

Sonia stepped forward, grasping her hands. "And then Bethany called all of us and we knew we had to drop everything and come over. We're so sorry, Reidun. You've been there for all of us, but we let you down."

"What about your husbands?" Reidun asked.

"They were okay with it. They know what you mean to us," Bethany said.

Johanna held up a grocery bag. "I brought food. Knowing you, I'll bet you've got nothing in this house but TV dinners, noodles, and knekkebrød."

Reidun laughed through her tears. "I don't know what to say."

Sonia pulled her into a hug. "You don't have to say anything. At least not yet. Just let us love on you, okay?" She stood back. "And then we want all the gory details. We need to know whether to beat up Steinar or not. I'm still not clear on that."

As they all went into the living room, it hit Reidun. While she'd been feeling so forgotten and abandoned and drowning in misery, God had been gathering her friends.

More tears came, but they were tears of gratitude.

Chapter Twenty-One

STEINAR PULLED HIS KEYS out of his pocket. The long walk back home from Bethany's place had set his mind clear on a number of things.

If there was going to be any chance for a relationship with Reidun, he needed to create the breathing space they needed.

And that meant Vivian had to go. He wasn't sure how. She'd never said how long she'd be staying. And he didn't want to ask her to leave. She was his children's aunt, and he didn't want to create a rift between them and their mother's family.

Turning the key in the lock, he breathed a prayer for wisdom.

He walked into the living room, freezing as he caught sight of Vivian.

She sat on the sofa, her small suitcase open next to her. "That must have been a very long walk. You've been gone for hours."

"It ended up being longer than I expected." He took a step closer, staring at the suitcase. "What are you doing?"

"While you were out, I found there's a flight that leaves town first thing tomorrow." She gave him a strained smile. "I'm going to be on it."

He sat on the edge of an armchair, relief making his legs weak. *Thank you, Lord! I didn't even have to tell her myself.* He fought to keep a grin from spreading across his face.

Vivian zipped her suitcase shut. "I won't ask you to see me to the airport because I know you have to stay with the children. But I hope you'll call me a taxi."

"Yes, of course." He threaded his fingers through his hair. "Why the sudden decision to leave?" He regretted the question. Maybe he shouldn't ask. She might decide to stay even longer.

She threw him a sidelong glance, a small smile curving her lips. "It was time."

"Vivian, I—"

"No need to say anything."

She put the suitcase on the floor and walked to the bookshelf. Her back still turned to Steinar, she picked up Charlotte's portrait. "You know, my sister was an exceptional woman."

Steinar stared at her in surprise. "Of course I know that."

"I looked up to her so much. And when I think of how she fought tooth and nail to get those children..."

"I know that, too," Steinar said. "I was there for every failed round of IVF and both miscarriages, remember? I wanted those children just as badly as Charlotte did."

Vivian spun around to face Steinar, her eyes hard. "Tell Reidun she'd better be good to them, or she'll have to answer to me."

Steinar stared at her. "What?"

Vivian put the portrait back and crossed her arms. "She's the one you're dating, isn't she?"

"Yes."

"I wish you'd told me that earlier. I might have—" she held up her hand and shook her head. "It doesn't matter now. Anyway, I promised Charlotte I'd watch over the twins, and I mean to keep that promise. So, make sure you tell Reidun that, okay?"

He nodded, unable to summon any words to reply.

"I'm going to bed now," she said. "Could you arrange a taxi for a five o'clock pickup?"

"Yes. You're leaving without saying bye to Chase and Mya? They get up early, but that's a stretch even for them."

"I'll call them when I get to England." She stood still and gave him a long look.

Finally, she broke eye contact. "Good night."

She walked halfway down the hall, then stopped and faced him. "Tell me one thing, Steinar. I'll only ask this once." She crossed her arms. "Was there ever a chance of something between you and me?"

Her question threw him. "No. No, there wasn't. I'm sorry if I ever gave you any other impression."

She raised her chin, her lips pressed together. "Okay. Fair enough. What is it about Reidun, then? What's so special about her? She's not your type at all."

"What's special about her?" How could he explain it to Vivian? He searched his heart for the words to capture Reidun's shining essence. "She's a woman of faith. She's strong. She's independent and tenacious. She fights for what she believes in even though she's scared she'll fail."

"I see. Well, that's nice to know."

Squaring her shoulders, she turned around and went into Mya's room.

Steinar remained where he stood. The truth was as clear as day. He loved

Reidun. How could he get her to see that?

Chapter Twenty-Two

22

EIDUN'S FOUR FRIENDS TALKED, cried, laughed, and prayed with her deep into the night, finally snatching a few hours of sleep wherever they found space in her guest bedroom and sofa.

When they went their separate ways for their various jobs the next morning, they left her with her heart full.

Picking up her phone after a quick shower, Reidun found a text message from Steinar.

Can I see you tonight?

She bit her lip. She didn't want to burst open the warm cocoon of comfort and love her friends had wrapped her in, but she had to face Steinar. They'd left things unresolved, and they needed to talk and figure out where their relationship stood.

She typed her reply.

Yes. Do you mind coming here? Six o'clock would be best.

When she opened the door later that evening, Steinar held two greenish brown drinks in lidded mason jars.

Reidun pointed, not quite believing her eyes. "Are those avocado and coffee milkshakes?"

"Yes. Your friend Johanna was kind enough to share her recipe with me."

She stepped aside to let him pass. "You brought those all the way from home?"

"I did." He handed one to her.

She took a long sip through her straw, enjoying the sweet, creamy blend. "Mm. How did you know that I love these?"

He smiled, watching her face. "Bethany told me."

The expression in his eyes made her heart flutter.

"I haven't stopped thinking about what happened on Monday afternoon at the bookshop," he said. "It opened my eyes to a lot of things, and I want you to know how seriously I'm taking it."

He raked a hand through his hair. "There's a reason I made you an avocado and coffee milkshake. I talked to your friend Bethany about us last night."

"She told me you met."

His eyebrows went up. "She did? Did she tell you about the milkshake?"

"No. What's the big deal about it?"

"When I told her we were dating, at first she was really surprised. She said she'd never have put the two of us together."

Reidun winced. "She told me that, too."

"She also said that when she thinks about us, we remind her of an avocado and coffee milkshake. Two things most people would never have thought to pair, but they work."

Her heart thudded at the intensity of his gaze.

"Reidun, I believe we work," he said, a tremor in his voice. "Like an avocado and coffee milkshake. I know you have your doubts, but it's true. You're not like any woman I've ever met. And I absolutely love that."

He stepped toward her, resting his hands gently on her shoulders. "Yes, I said love."

Her pulse thundered in her ears.

"You're smart, strong, funny, and beautiful. You're generous and kind. My children think you're the ultimate level of cool, and I do, too. I love you, Reidun. But I haven't forgotten about what happened at the bookshop. My behavior frightened and hurt you, and it disgusted and frightened me, too. Earlier today, I made an appointment with a therapist. I want to understand what happened and do the work I need to do on myself. I'll do it whatever you decide about us. I just wanted to let you know that."

His hands slid off her shoulders, and he stepped away from her. "I'm not going to pressure you. I only wanted to lay all my cards on the table."

He said "no pressure" but she knew he wanted a response. She felt light-headed. "I'm... I'm scared," she said. "I keep thinking, do you really know me well enough to love me? What if you get closer and find I'm not who you think I am, and your feelings change? What if I'm not enough for you?"

Her heart ached as his eyes glistened. "I'm sorry," she whispered.

His voice was husky. "I guess it's too soon. But I wanted you to know how I feel. Would you... Would you be willing to take things slowly, in case there's a chance you might come to feel how I do?"

"That's the thing. I already feel how you do," she said. "That's why I'm so scared."

He crossed the distance between them in one step. "You love me?"

She nodded. "But I'm a big, fat coward."

He lifted his hand to her face, cupping her cheek in his palm. "If it's any consolation, I'm scared, too. I'm scared of hurting you again. I'm scared of losing you. Love always comes with the risk of loss. The only way I can love you, or my children, and not go insane with fear is to trust that God loves us even more, and will take care of us no matter what."

Her heart swelled within her, and she understood. He was as scared as she was. Maybe even more, because he knew the agony of loss. But he was still willing to put his heart on the line again and choose to love her.

Sliding her hands up his chest, she decided to defy her fear and take that leap of faith. With him. And with the God who loved them both.

She raised herself on her toes and kissed him. He responded instantly, returning her kiss with exquisite tenderness. She felt like she was freefalling, an exhilarating blend of joy and wonder.

He wrapped her in his arms, and she rested her head on his shoulder. Someone's heart was beating wildly. She didn't know whether it was hers or his.

His lips grazed her forehead. "Are you still scared?"

She pulled him closer. "A bit. But I'm just imagining you have a rubber chicken on your head."

His chest rumbled with laughter, and he kissed her again.

Epilogue

Thirteen Months Later

THE SMELL OF ROASTING chestnuts tinged the crisp winter air and set Reidun's stomach rumbling as she rearranged the wooden candlesticks in her craft stall. Thankfully, Chase and Steinar should be back soon with some hot chocolate.

Berghaven's town square, blanketed with fresh snow, was transformed into a winter wonderland for the second annual Christmas Fair.

Although they were in the middle of the dark time of the year, the night skies only made the festive lights glow brighter.

"How much for this bowl?" An elderly woman in a black coat wore her red beret at a jaunty angle. She pointed at a chunky pine fruit bowl.

Reidun hid a smile as Mya answered. "It's two hundred kroner. But you can get this full set of three for three hundred and fifty. It's a much better deal. My stepmother made them by hand from reclaimed wood."

It still amazed her how well the twins spoke Norwegian now. It was impossible to tell that they hadn't been born and raised in Berghaven.

The customer smiled. "Is that so? Well, because you're such a good salesgirl, I'll get the three bowls. Where do I pay?"

Reidun raised her hand. "Over here. I'll wrap them for you. Are you paying by card or cash?"

"Cash, please," the woman said. She nodded at Mya. "That's your step-daughter, eh? Lovely child. You're doing a wonderful job."

"Thank you, but her mother and my husband deserve the credit. I just get to reap the rewards." Reidun folded layers of tissue paper around the three bowls. "Is this your first visit to the Berghaven Christmas fair?"

"No, I came for the first one last year. It's wonderful. It's such a nice atmosphere compared to the one at Havdal. Much better organized, too. I can't imagine why they never had one before."

Reidun glowed with delight as she put the bowls into a paper bag and slipped in a business card. "I hope you'll come again next year. Here are your bowls and your change. Merry Christmas."

"Merry Christmas," the woman replied. "And merry Christmas to you, too, little girl."

Mya turned to Reidun. "Mamma, I just sold the last bowls. Do I get a bonus?"

Reidun's heart always melted when the twins called her Mamma. Their own mother remained "Mummy" in

English, so Reidun had never felt like she was usurping Charlotte's place in their hearts. They had only one "Mummy" but now they had a "Mamma" as well.

"Did someone say bonus?" Steinar and Chase came up to the stall holding hot drinks and snacks.

"Mya just sold the last bowls, and we were negotiating her bonus. And Chase gets one, too, for selling that chess set."

She pulled two one hundred kroner notes from her purse and handed one to each of the children.

"Nice." Chase took his money with a grin. "Can we go skating now?"

Reidun said, "Let's all go after I pack up. I've sold almost all my stock and I want to chill out."

As they packed up the remaining merchandise, Sonia came jogging up to the stall. "There you are. Mya, Chase, the children's gingerbread house competition is about to start. Didn't you want to join in?"

"Oh no, I forgot," Chase said. "We were going to the skating rink after Dad and Mamma pack up."

Sonia looked at Steinar. "I could take them for the competition while you finish packing up, and you can go skating then. It's a timed competition and will only last fifteen minutes."

"That sounds good. Do you two want to go with Sonia?"

The children nodded enthusiastically and trotted away.

Reidun sighed as they went.

Steinar slid his arms around her waist and kissed her ear. "What was that sigh about?"

She turned around in his arms and returned his hug. "It was a happy sigh. God has blessed us so much."

"He has, indeed." Steinar bent his head forward and kissed her, breaking away when someone cleared their throat in front of the stall.

She spun around to see Oskar and his wife Elsa.

Elsa smirked. "Looks like someone's found the mistletoe. Hello, Reidun. Steinar."

"Hello," Steinar said, keeping his arms around Reidun.

Oskar inclined his head. "I must congratulate you both. I've just been looking at the preliminary numbers, and this fair has already smashed last year's foot traffic and revenue numbers, and it's only the first day."

"Is that so?" Steinar said. "That's fantastic news, Reidun."

"It is indeed." Oskar looked from Reidun to Steinar. "I'm always the first one to admit when I'm wrong. On any count. So, I have to congratulate you both."

The men exchanged a long glance that Reidun couldn't read.

Then Oskar said, "We'd better be going. Merry Christmas."

"Merry Christmas," Reidun replied.

She shivered as she watched them go.

Steinar's arms tightened around her. "Are you cold?"

"No." She leaned against his chest. "I was just thinking that if I'd gotten what I wanted twenty-five odd years ago, I would have been married to Oskar."

"In Chase's eloquent words, ew."

Reidun laughed. Ew, indeed.

"So, was I worth the wait?" Steinar asked.

"One hundred percent."

The End

Titles by Milla Holt

COLOR-BLIND LOVE SERIES

Falling for the Foe

Pushing Past the Pain

Lessons Learned in Love

Hidden in Her Heart

Last Flight Home

ALL THINGS NEW: A MOSAIC
ANTHOLOGY

Lost and Found

A THRILL IN THE AIR: A MOSAIC
ANTHOLOGY

The Prodigal's Feast

SEASONS OF FAITH SERIES

Into the Flood

Through the Blaze

Within the Storm

Amid the Ashes

After the Frost

About the Author

I write fiction that reflects my Christian faith. I love happy endings, heroes and heroines who discover sometimes hard but always vital truths, and stories that uplift and encourage.

My family and I live in the east of England where we enjoy rambling in the countryside, reading good books and making up silly lyrics to our favorite songs.

To learn about my other books, join my mailing list, and grab a free exclusive book, visit my website at www.millaholt.com